WINGS & DESTRUCTION

THE VAMPIRE AND ANGEL WARS BOOK ONE

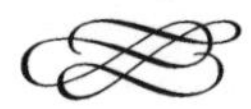

G.K. DE ROSA

ISBN: 978-1720034025

Cover Designer: Sanja Gombar www.fantasybookcoverdesign.com

Published in 2018 by G.K. DeRosa LLC
Palm Beach, Florida
www.gkderosa.com

Created with Vellum

To the very first person that bought my debut novel, whoever you are, thank you!

~ G.K. De Rosa

CONTENTS

CHAPTER 1

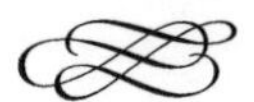

Winged-beasts circled the dark sky overhead, the flapping of their enormous wings creating an incessant drone. It buzzed across my eardrums twenty-four/seven, a constant torture. Maybe that was their plan—to wait for the remaining humans to go insane. I stared out of the little basement window with my hands over my ears. When would the angels leave? It had been weeks since the fighting ended and still they remained.

This was vampire territory now. A chill slithered up my spine as the terrible image that flooded my nightmares coalesced in the forefront of my mind. My dead parents. Murdered like more than half of the adults in the country. Sometimes I wished they'd killed me too.

A cold nose squirmed its way under my arm and buried itself in my lap. I cracked a smile and rubbed behind Duke's big ears. He whimpered, and I pushed the dark thoughts away. Somehow he always knew when I needed him most. "I don't know what I'd do without you, buddy."

He barked, and I quickly shushed him. Vampires and angels had heightened hearing. They had heightened everything. The only reason we'd survived this long was because we lived on a remote farm in upstate New York. The fighting started in the big cities, and one by one each large metropolis in the country fell. You'd think in a war between angels and vampires one side would've killed the other off.

You'd be wrong.

Instead, it was the human population that ended up nearly decimated.

Both sides were much too powerful, and neither would surrender. They ravaged cities in golden fire and pools of crimson blood. In the end, there were no winners. Not really anyway. They split the country along the fortieth parallel dividing their spoils in half. The vampires got the north including New York City, and the angels got Washington D.C. and the remaining southern half.

One thing was certain: the humans lost.

A light knock at the basement door sent my heart rate skyrocketing. Duke bared his fangs, and a low growl reverberated in his throat. I jumped up and blew out the candle on my makeshift bedside table. I put my index finger to my lips and shot Duke a narrowed glare. The growling stopped, and he fell to my side as I crept toward the door.

I crouched at the foot of the stairs as sweat trickled down my back. Two more knocks and a long pause. My shoulders sagged, and I released the breath I'd been holding.

"It's me, open up," a familiar voice hissed through the metal door.

I lifted the lever to release the deadlock and heaved the door open. If my dad hadn't had this old door fortified when things started to get bad, I would've never survived this long.

Emerald green eyes peered in through the doorway. "You gotta be more careful, Liv. I could see the candlelight through the window as I got closer."

My best friend padded down the stairs and ran a hand over his buzzed dark blonde hair.

"You only saw it because you knew it was there, Asher."

"Maybe. But I only have normal human vision—unlike the others." His eyes veered up toward the sky. "I want you to be careful. Especially when I'm not around."

I placed my hands on my hips and stared up at my friend. At six foot one, he had to duck when moving through certain parts of the basement. I had no such problems. I may have been tall for a girl, but luckily I fit just fine in the safe house my dad had built. "Why are you back so soon? I thought you weren't returning till tomorrow." I picked up the candle and moved it further away from the one window, re-lighting it.

He shrugged, and a dark shadow fell over his bright irises. "There's nothing out there, Liv. I went as far as Thompson's farm, and there wasn't a scrap left."

I glanced at the bare metal shelves along the dark wall. The utter emptiness mirrored the sensation in my chest—and my stomach. Only a handful of cans remained. We'd survived on our stock of supplies for almost six months, but if we didn't find more soon, we were screwed. I plopped down on the floor and Asher sat across from me, the reflection of the candle's flame dancing in his eyes.

Angels and vampires didn't need food to survive so they didn't care that they destroyed everything edible during the war. The vampires took humans as hostages and turned them into blood slaves so they had all they needed. They created slave camps all along the north to sate their blood lust. New York City was their capital—Grand Central Station the seat of their throne. No one knew how many humans were still alive and enslaved. Everyone had lost someone in the past year, and the worst part was not knowing if they were even alive.

I guessed I was lucky I knew. Even luckier I hadn't seen my parents' horrific fate with my own eyes. Only Asher bore that burden.

"We'll have to go farther out to search," I finally said. My parents died six months ago to protect me, and I wouldn't let their sacrifice be in vain. I couldn't give up, no matter how much I wanted to sometimes.

"You're not going anywhere." He reached out for my hand and squeezed. "It's not safe."

I jerked it out of his grasp. I hated when he treated me like a little girl he had to protect. Asher was eighteen, not even a full year older than me, but he always treated me like a kid sister. "It's not safe for you either, and you still went."

"Well, I can't just sit here and let us starve."

"Neither can I." I tucked a wave of dark hair behind my ear and gave him my best steely gaze. "We'll go tomorrow morning—all of us." I wouldn't leave Duke behind either.

He shook his head, his lips pressed together in a thin line. "You haven't been out there in weeks, Liv. You don't know what it's like."

I got to my feet and approached the small window, blades of brown grass obstructing my view. The sky was completely dark now, but the steady droning continued. "Maybe it's time I did."

CHAPTER 2

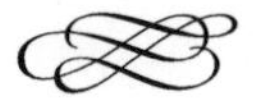

I rolled over on the cot and jabbed my elbow into the cold metal frame, sending a sharp tingle all the way up my arm. I clenched my jaw to suppress the curse on the tip of my tongue. No matter how many nights I'd slept on this uncomfortable thing, I didn't think I'd ever get used to it. I swore I had hit my funny bone at least once a week for the past year.

Dad had made us move down here as soon as things got bad. He was smart. The surrounding farms didn't fare as well, my best friend's included. I rolled back over, and bright green eyes locked onto mine.

"Sorry, did I wake you?" he whispered.

"No. It was this poor excuse for a bed." The sun never rose anymore; the sky was always covered in dark clouds, which made it difficult to figure out when to wake up. Luckily, my wristwatch still worked. I checked the time and grunted. "Why are you up so early? It's barely five."

He shrugged and ran his hand over his short hair. "I couldn't sleep."

His cot was across the way from mine; if I reached out I could've touched his nose. Something made me want to, but the hollow look in his eye stopped me. "Everything's going to be fine, Ash. We'll find food today and we'll survive, just like we have for the past months."

He swung his long legs over the side of the crude bed and sat up. "I don't know. Something's changed since the war ended. It's like the vamps and angels are working together. That's only going to make things worse for us."

I sat up too and met his gaze with a fiery one of my own. "Don't you give up on us, Asher St. John. I need you. We're all we have left."

He wrapped his fingers around the edge of the cot and squeezed. His eyes were shiny, and I knew his thoughts were on his family. I averted my gaze to give him a second. He lost his parents and little sister early on. His farm was a few miles from here and had somehow gotten caught in the middle of the early fighting. An orange ball of fire had decimated the entire place in minutes taking his whole family with it. Asher would've been dead too if he hadn't been visiting me that day. Before the world went to hell, I thought there could be more than just friendship between us. Then everything happened, and our feelings got buried in the ash along with everything else.

He cleared his throat and shot up to his feet. "Since we're up, we might as well get an early start."

I followed his lead and began to gather my belongings for the trek. We had no idea how far we'd have to go to find food, so I piled all of our remaining cans and bottled water on the floor and divided them between the two backpacks.

Asher knelt down beside me and grabbed a few extra cans from my pack and threw them in his. "There's no way you're carrying that much when I'm twice you're size."

I arched a brow. "I can pull my own weight, Ash. When we're out there, I need you to know that."

He nodded, and my eyes veered to the window. It wasn't full dark anymore; tiny hints of light shone through the clouds. No one was sure how they did it, but somehow the vampires had managed to block the sun. Maybe it was a rumor, but what other explanation was there? I wondered if things were different in the south. Or in the rest of the world. Without a working communication system, we'd lost touch with the outside.

I packed the remaining bit of dog food and snapped on Duke's leash. His black tail whipped furiously from side to side. Poor guy really missed the outdoors. Before, he had the run of the farm. He'd spend the day chasing pigs and shepherding the sheep. Now he was only allowed out twice a day for a quick bathroom break. I'm surprised he hadn't gone completely stir crazy. German shepherds weren't meant to be cooped up in a small space like this.

Neither were humans.

"Looks like Duke's excited." I slid the backpack on my shoulder.

"That makes one of us," Asher muttered. He moved to the old wooden chest in the corner and flipped the lid up.

"You're taking that?"

He reached in and pulled out my dad's gun. "Just in case."

"Bullets aren't going to stop angels or vampires."

"It might not stop them, but it'll slow them down. And anyway, it's not just for them."

I chewed my lower lip. The worst part about war was what it did to people. It brought out the worst in most. Looters ran rampant now that there was no police force to stop them. Some would kill for a bottle of water. I hated to admit it, but Asher was right. We'd need that gun to protect ourselves from other humans.

I pushed the depressing thoughts aside as he grabbed a few rounds of ammunition and stuck them in his backpack. "Which way should we go?"

He pulled a crumpled map from his back pocket and held it out by the candle. "This is where I got to yesterday." He traced his finger along the blue line. "We could try heading further north instead. There will be fewer chances of running into angels or vamps, but it's also less populated so less chance of large food supplies."

"And if we go south?"

"More people, more food and more of *them*."

Neither sounded great. I mulled over the two options in my mind. "Let's go south."

"That's going to be riskier."

"You said yourself there was nothing where you went yesterday. If we go further north we're probably going to find the same. We need to go where humans are. People mean food and maybe even safety."

He folded the map and shoved it back in his pocket. "Fine." He tightened the straps on his backpack and trudged to the door. "You ready?"

I nodded and took a step in front of him. His fingers wrapped around my arm, and he pulled me back. "Ouch!" I squealed.

"Sorry." He loosened his grip but didn't let go. "When we're out there, you stay by my side at all times, you got it?"

"I got it." I motioned for him to go first and shot him my most sarcastic smile.

He slid the steel bar over and heaved the door open. The flapping of wings intensified the moment I poked my head out. I glanced up to get a better look at them. The angels. They were supposed to be good. They were supposed to protect humankind. No one really understood what had gone wrong.

Lowering my gaze, my eyes landed on the sorry remnants of my home. Charred wooden beams were all that remained after seventeen years of happy memories.

"No time for gawking." Asher yanked my arm and dragged me past the dry pond, toward the apple orchards.

Or what used to be the apple orchards. Miles of burnt trees stretched before us. They didn't provide great cover, but it was better than nothing.

"We'll follow the path to Sanson's farm and see if there's

anything left of it. It's been a few months since I've been down that way."

"Okay." I hurried to match Asher's pace, his long legs eating up the scorched earth beneath us. Duke strolled beside me, his tongue hanging out of his mouth. I could've sworn he was smiling.

The steady flap of gigantic wings buzzed in my eardrums as we marched on. The constant noise steam-rolled over everything else. I'd walked through these orchards hundreds of times as a kid, and they were always full of life—birds singing, insects chirping, and the hum of tractors at work. Now it seemed dead. Except for that damn flapping.

I sighed and tried to pretend things were like they used to be. If I squinted my eyes just right, I could envision bright red apples dotting vibrant green trees instead of the bare sickly brown ones.

"What's wrong?" Ash turned his gaze on me.

I huffed. "Everything."

A shadow of a smile pulled at his lips, and for a second I was reminded of the cute boy I used to know. The guy that stood before me now may have looked like him, but he was harder, darker.

"Do you remember when I taught you to climb a tree?"

I grinned. "You mean when you broke my arm?"

He chuckled. "Don't exaggerate. It was only a sprain." He pointed down the row. "It was that one right over there."

"Really?" I jogged over to the tree he had indicated, Duke nipping at my heels. I tilted my head up. "It seemed much taller in my mind."

"Maybe you were that much shorter." He smirked and leaned up against the rough, brittle bark and exhaled a long breath.

I nudged him in the shoulder and sidled next to him. "Even though you almost killed me, I was the best climber of all the girls in my class."

"Oh, I remember. And it wasn't only trees you'd climb. I recall a certain escape attempt from your second floor bedroom."

I laughed. I'd forgotten all about that. My dad grounded me for a week for that one. "That was your fault too! I just wanted to go hunting with you and Crowder. Dad didn't think it was proper for a young lady."

"He was probably right."

My chest tightened. I'd give anything to be grounded again as long as it meant my parents were still here.

"Come on, we have to keep going." Asher's fingers wrapped around my hand, and he led me back onto the worn path.

After what felt like days, we finally reached Sanson's farm. Or what was left of it. The roof had been completely torn off, and the remainder looked more like a dollhouse than a farmhouse. We had a bird's eye view of every single room. The porch and front side of the house had been ripped clean off.

Asher's shoulders sagged as he stared at the ruined structure. "I was hoping maybe Mr. Sanson and the girls were still here."

I squeezed his hand. "Maybe they got out."

"Doubtful," he muttered.

Duke barked and took off toward the broken old house. I yelled after him, but whatever he'd caught scent of was more enticing. We ran after him as he circled around behind the house.

A small red silo still stood intact. Duke pawed at the door, his tail wagging.

"Maybe there's something inside?"

A steel padlock remained firmly in place. Asher jiggled the lock, but it was locked tight. He got up on his tiptoes and ran his hand over the doorframe.

"Aha!" He held up the small silver key triumphantly. "I guess my dad wasn't the only one with such a predictable hiding spot."

"Thank goodness for small miracles."

He wiggled the key into the padlock, and it clicked open. Duke stuck his nose in and led the way. I flicked on my flashlight and lit up the small circular space. A black blur scurried across the ground, and I screamed. Duke took off after it as it ran behind bales of hay.

"Damn it." Ash's eyes scanned the silo.

Nothing but hay and a lone rat. "Well I guess that's what had Duke excited."

"I'm not ready to eat a rat yet, you?"

Bleh. "Definitely not." I pointed my flashlight at Duke, and big brown eyes glowed in the dark. A skinny rat hung out of his mouth. *So gross.* At least I could keep what was left of the dog food for tomorrow.

"Come on." Ash held the door open, and I trudged out.

Two rifles pointed at my head, a man at the end of each. I gasped and Asher yanked my arm, pulling me behind him. Duke barked like mad, his hackles raised.

"Shut that dog up or I will," said a scruffy-bearded man.

I grabbed Duke's collar and forced him down to the ground.

"We don't want no trouble," said the taller one. "Give us your supplies, and we'll be on our way."

"Not happening," Asher growled as he slid one strap off his shoulder.

He was going for the gun. I knew he was, and he was going to get killed for it. Two rifles against one gun wasn't a fair fight.

I held my hands up, my heart lodged in my throat. "I'll give you everything I have, just please let us keep one pack." I shot the two grimy men my best puppy dog eyes, praying they'd buy it. "Please."

The taller man nodded at scruffy beard, and they both lowered their weapons. I quickly unzipped my bag and dumped out all of its contents. Scruffy beard bent down to pick up the cans and bottles, and from my periphery I noticed Ash's hand twitch. I shot him a narrowed glare, slowly shaking my head.

It wasn't worth it.

The man straightened, shoving all of our supplies into a duffel bag. “Nice doin’ business with you two.” They took off at a sprint toward the woods, half of our supplies in tow.

“Dammit, Liv.” Asher kicked the ground, sending a cloud of dirt up into the air. “You should’ve let me try to stop them.”

“Absolutely not. You could’ve gotten yourself killed.” I zipped up my empty backpack and slid it back on my shoulders. “At least you had most of the food.”

He ground his teeth together. “It’s not enough.”

“We’ll find more. At least we’re all still alive.” I patted his arm, his muscles tense. “Come on, let’s get out of here.”

He took the map out and scanned it. “Ten more miles and we’ll hit the outskirts of the suburbs. You’re sure that’s where you want to go? Running into more people might not necessarily be a good thing.”

I nodded. “We have to try.”

CHAPTER 3

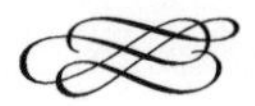

Every single muscle in my body screamed for me to stop. To put an end to the torture. I ignored them and marched on. In another hour it would be full dark, and we'd have to stop. If we didn't reach Fallsbrooke, that meant a night in the woods.

"Just a little farther." Ash wrapped his arm around my waist and tugged me along.

I was practically sleepwalking as it was. In the distance, the spotty lights of the valley called out to me tauntingly. Lights meant electricity, which meant hot water. We'd lost all of that months ago. I'd kill for a hot shower right about now.

Asher pulled me to the edge of the hill. "It's all downhill from here. Another hour, and we'll be back in civilization."

I peered down at the suburban communities sprawled before us. There could be humans down there. Hope blossomed in my chest. I swallowed hard and buried it down, not wanting to be disappointed. I couldn't bear it if we were wrong.

"Okay. Let's do this." I gritted my teeth and ignored the knives piercing my feet with every step. Even Duke looked tired. His big tongue hung out of his mouth, his breaths coming short. I took a sip from our dwindling water supply then stopped to offer him a cup. He lapped it up greedily then cocked his head when he finished. "Sorry, buddy. That's all for now." I picked up the mug, and we continued onward.

The woods were quiet. We hadn't encountered a single soul, alive or otherwise along our journey so far. I wasn't sure if I should be happy or worried about that.

"How are you holding up?" asked Asher.

"Oh you know, just great." I plastered a fake smile on my face. "How about you?"

"I could definitely use a bed right about now."

"Yeah, no kidding." I glanced up at my best friend and wondered what I looked like. Dark circles rimmed his eyes, and a mix of sweat and dirt covered his face. The crazy part was that he still looked good. Underneath the layer of grime, sun-kissed skin and bright green eyes shone through. Years of working on his family farm had produced perfectly tanned skin and long lean muscles.

"Why are you looking at me like that?"

"Like what?" Heat rose to my cheeks as he regarded me with those darting emerald eyes. I'd never seen an emerald in person, but it was my birthstone and I'd always dreamed of owning one. He was the closest I'd ever get.

"Like I'm a tasty slice of pizza."

I laughed. "Maybe because I'm starving." I reached for his face and wiped a smudge of dirt from his cheek. "And because you had a little something on your face." My hand lingered on his cheek for a minute longer than it should have.

"Thanks," he muttered and covered my hand with his, pressing it into his cheek.

His heated skin warmed my palm, his stubble tickling my hand. His eyes locked onto mine, and my breath hitched.

Duke let out a loud bark.

Asher's eyes widened, and he yanked me down to the ground.

We scurried to the nearest tree and pressed our bodies flat up against it. The crunch of leaves and twigs snapping drew my attention a few yards to our left. Two figures raced through the woods, darting between trees.

Just over the treetops, three angels flew by. Their large wings flapped, rustling the branches overhead. Duke tilted his nose upward and growled.

"Shh!"

He whined and lowered his head to the ground.

I held my breath, my eyes fixed overhead as the three angels circled the sky. It was too dark to see much, but their wings emitted a soft glow. It was just enough to be able to follow their path.

"Are those nephilim?" I whispered.

"I think so. Their wings seem a little smaller."

"Do you think they saw those people?"

He nodded, pressing his lips together.

I gulped. Nephilim were the angel's warriors on earth. They were half-human, half-divine and totally deadly. I still didn't understand why the vampires allowed angels in their territory. They should've all been gone by now. Then again, I wasn't sure which I preferred—death by angel or vampire. On the bright side, the angels would probably just kidnap me and make me their slave. The vampires on the other hand would suck me dry.

"I think they're gone." Asher's quiet voice pulled me from my dismal thoughts.

I released a breath and sat up. "Do you really think the angels are still capturing humans to serve them?

He shrugged.

"How many freakin' servants do they need?"

"I don't know, but I heard they built a massive tower in D.C. as their headquarters. Rumors are that it stretches all the way to heaven."

I frowned. "These angels don't belong in heaven."

"I don't think there are any left in heaven anymore. They're all here on earth, ruining the world for the rest of us." He plucked a dry blade of grass and stuck it in his mouth. It looked like a cigarette, hanging from his bottom lip. "What kind of God would let this happen?"

"God had nothing to do with this."

Fury flashed across his irises. "How's that possible? Angels are God's messengers aren't they?"

I clenched my jaw. I *so* wasn't having this argument with him again. We'd both been brought up Catholic, and the angels we'd heard about our whole lives were nothing like these terrible creatures that flew around ravaging everything in their path. There was no way God intended any of this.

"Well?"

"I'm not talking to you about this for the umpteenth time. Something must have gone wrong. Maybe they're fallen angels..."

"All of them?"

I shook my head and got back to my feet. My legs screamed in protest. "Come on. It's almost full dark, and I don't want to be out here with *them* flying around."

We trudged on for the next half hour without speaking or even looking at each other. Ash could be so stubborn sometimes; he drove me crazy. The silence too was driving me crazy. If it weren't for the constant hum of angel wings, I would've started humming the latest Shawn Mendes song. It had been months since the radio stations stopped playing, but I couldn't get that last one out of my head.

The thick maze of trees began to grow sparser, and the woods gave way to a paved road.

"I-95," said Asher as he stared at the highway in front of us. A cement barrier separated it from the encroaching woods. On the opposite side was a walled-in housing development. The first one we'd seen in miles.

"We made it!" Tears blurred my vision. I never thought I'd be so happy to see some generic beige houses.

Ash peered to the left then the right. He was being overly cautious. There wasn't a car in sight. He hopped over the barrier and held out his hand to help me. I climbed over, and Duke followed behind. We ran across the highway, completely out in the open. When we reached the other side we crouched down next to the wall.

I glanced up at the imposing ten-foot partition. It might as well have been a hundred. "How're we getting over that?"

"We're not. We're going under." He looked at Duke and smiled.

Duke was a master digger. There wasn't a fence that could hold him in. If he couldn't jump over it, he'd just dig under it. For once, it was going to come in handy. I turned to my dog and patted the ground. "Get it, buddy. Get it!"

With Duke's strong claws and a bit of our help, we had a nice German shepherd sized hole in about fifteen minutes.

"I'll go first. I'm bigger than both of you, so if I can make it, you two should be fine."

I nodded and Asher went head first into the tunnel. The wall wasn't wide, a few feet at most, but I still held my breath until I heard his voice on the other side.

"Okay your turn."

"I can't. I have to make sure Duke gets through first."

"Fine," he hissed.

I pushed Duke's nose down the hole and after a little objecting, he squirmed his way through.

Loud wings flapping overhead snapped my attention to the sky. *Crap*! It must have been the three nephilim we saw earlier.

"Go, Liv, now!" shouted Asher.

CHAPTER 4

I dove into the hole and crawled through the narrow tunnel. Rocks and pointy debris scratched my knees and palms as I squirmed through the darkness. I refused to think about all the spiders that I must have been squishing. Long arms appeared at the end of the tunnel, and I grabbed onto warm hands.

I didn't even have time to dust myself off before Asher yanked me to a full out run. The flutter of wings above us sent my heart rate skyrocketing. We raced around the corner of a large beige house. Apparently, we'd dug right into someone's backyard.

"We have to get inside," whisper-shouted Asher over his shoulder.

"There!" I pointed at the house next door. The sliding glass door was smashed in, providing a muddied view into their living room.

We hurried across the yard to the other house, Duke running beside me. Asher went straight for the door, ignoring the shards of glass protruding from the doorframe. I jumped through the gaping hole and crunched through cracked glass on the floor. I nearly ran right into Asher's back. He'd frozen as soon as he'd leapt inside.

He turned to me with his index finger to his lips. He took a step, and glass crackled underneath his shoe. He put his hand up and motioned for me to stay put. I grabbed Duke by the collar and didn't move. I hoped he hadn't cut up his paws with all the glass. If he weren't so big I'd try to carry him, but considering he weighed as much as I did, it was impossible.

I chewed on my fingernails as Asher tiptoed around the house. I held my breath as he disappeared around the corner. A thick blanket of black surrounded me. I couldn't even hear Ash's footsteps anymore. My heartbeat roared across my eardrums, drowning out Duke's panting. Why was he taking so long?

Asher's blonde head poked around the corner, and the tightness in my chest abated. He pulled the flashlights out of his backpack, handing me the extra one and pointed it toward the floor. "The place is empty."

"Good," I breathed.

"There's a bedroom down that hall. Grab a sheet off the bed and I'm going to see if I can find some tape to cover the sliding door."

I nodded and clicked my flashlight on. I crept down the hallway to the first door on the right. Vibrant framed landscapes hung on clean white walls. I had to restrain myself from jumping on the king sized bed. All I wanted to do was curl up into the soft comforter and not wake up until the sun came out. I hated to strip the mattress of the silky sheets, but I had to.

Duke watched me, his head cocked to the side, as I pulled the top sheet off. Before I went back into the living room, I checked his paws. Somehow he'd managed to avoid the glass. Thank goodness.

Asher was already standing by the broken glass door with a roll of masking tape. I handed him the sheet, and we got to work.

"The house is pretty stocked. Whoever lived here left in a hurry." He held the sheet as I taped it up.

"Did you find food?"

"Not a ton, but the pantry has some bottles of water and a whole shelf of canned goods."

"Any ramen?"

He chuckled. "That stuff is so bad for you."

"Oh right, like that's what's going to kill me."

He grunted and raked his hand over his spikey hair. "Don't joke about dying, Liv. Not now."

"Lighten up, Ash. We did good. We made it south, we survived looters, we gave those angels the slip, and we even found a nice place with food."

"I don't think we gave anyone the slip. They must've had better prey to hunt than us. And where there are three angels, there are surely more."

"How about the vampires? Where do you think they are?"

His lips twisted down, and I snapped my jaw closed. I really needed to learn to keep my mouth shut.

"They come out at night," he muttered.

I'd heard the same thing. Even though they'd found a way to keep the sun from shining, they still preferred to be out at night. I guessed the legends were true: they mostly slept during the day. The Stryx, their vampire-human hybrids, patrolled while they snoozed. They were even scarier than the vampires in my opinion. They were too humanlike. Apparently, vampires and humans had been intermingling for decades without anyone knowing. But how was it even possible? Some say the angels helped the vampires create them. Why was anyone's guess.

I secured the last piece of tape and turned to the kitchen. "Dinner?"

"Yes, please," he growled.

I raided the pantry and put together a scrumptious meal of cold beef stew, canned low-sodium peas and lukewarm bottled water by candlelight. It would've been kind of romantic in another world. We both dug in like it was a dinner at a five-star restaurant. I shoveled the stew into my mouth and had to restrain myself from groaning in pleasure.

Asher's eyes twinkled across from me. "If I would've known you were such a cheap date, I would've asked you out a long time ago."

I coughed, nearly choking on a mouthful of peas. "What?" I mumbled.

He shrugged, and I could've sworn his cheeks reddened but it was hard to tell in the dim light. "Nothing. I just wish things could've been different."

Yeah, no kidding. We finished the rest of the meal in silence. My mind was racing; I couldn't get it to quiet down. I'd known Asher practically my whole life. I'd had a crush on him for as long as I could remember, but I always thought he only considered me a kid sister. Except for right before all of this went down. Talk about bad timing.

"Go get some rest." Asher squeezed my shoulder and ticked his head toward the bedroom.

"How about you?"

"I'll keep watch."

"You have to sleep too, Ash. How are you going to protect us from all those *things* out there if you're too exhausted to keep your eyes open?" I took his hand and pulled him off the chair. "Duke can keep watch. Right, boy?"

Duke raised his head and whined.

Asher grinned. "Fine, but only for a few hours."

I led him down the hall to the bedroom I'd found before. The king size bed would be a huge upgrade to the hard cots we'd been used to. I crawled into the bed and sank into the mattress. I let out a quiet moan. It felt amazing on my sore muscles.

Asher chuckled and sat on the armchair across from the bed.

I picked up my head. "What are you doing?"

"Um, trying to sleep?"

"On the chair?"

He ran his hand over the back of his neck. "Yeah, this way I'll be more alert. Just in case."

I rolled my eyes and patted the empty side of the mattress next to me. "Come on, Ash. We've slept in the same bed like a million times."

"Yeah, when we were twelve."

I clapped my hand over my mouth so he couldn't see my smile. I couldn't believe I was making Asher St. John uncomfortable. "Get over here now."

He pushed himself up from the chair and slunk over to the other side of the bed.

I rolled over to face him as he crept under the covers. "Now is that so bad?"

He stretched, reaching his arms over his head and yawned. His biceps strained against his tight t-shirt. "No, I guess not." He turned toward me. "What are we going to do tomorrow?"

"I don't know. Maybe we stay here for a while. There's food and decent shelter—"

"And angels and nephilim crawling all over the place," he interrupted.

My gaze lifted to meet his. "Let's just enjoy this one night, okay?"

His eyes darkened and something flickered to life in his irises. His arm shot around my waist, and he pulled me into his chest. My breath hitched as the air between us crackled with intensity. His lips crashed into mine, and I gasped. He parted my lips with his tongue, and a fire ignited in my core. My brain struggled to make sense of what was happening, but my heart told it to shut up. He pressed me into his torso, his hands running up and down my back. My own hands lay frozen at my sides. I think they were in shock.

Just as quickly as the kissing started, it stopped. He pulled away, and it was like a bucket of ice had been poured over my head. I looked up at him, my brows knitted together. He wrapped his arms around me and squeezed. "Goodnight, Liv." He kissed the top of my head and within seconds, his breathing slowed and he was asleep.

Seriously?

CHAPTER 5

Asher St. John kissed me. After fifteen years of wondering what his lips tasted like, I now knew. Hope. It was cheesy, I knew, but that kiss gave me something I'd been missing for almost a year. Now he was acting like nothing had happened. I touched my lips, the memory of the kiss seared into them. No, I definitely hadn't dreamt it.

I wrapped the towel around my chest and ran my finger over the light pink birthmark over my heart. It was shaped like a heart, and my mom had always said it made me special. Who else got to where their heart on the outside? I smiled at the memory of her words.

After a day of trekking through the woods, the shower had felt amazing, even if it was cold. I should've taken it last night, but I'd been way too tired. I stared at my reflection in the mirror, realizing it was the first time I'd gotten a good look at myself in months. The basement hadn't been equipped with little luxuries like full-length mirrors. My cheeks seemed hollower, and I swore my collarbone was more pronounced than it used to be. Even my golden eyes seemed to have lost their fire, replaced by a dull hazel. A bitter laugh tumbled out as I remembered all the times I'd wanted to lose weight before. I should've done the one-can-of-food-a-day diet years ago.

A soft knock drew me away from my reflection.

I opened the door a crack and peeked through. Asher's bright eyes immediately dropped to the towel hastily wrapped around my wet body.

My pulse quickened.

His eyes widened for a second before he averted them back to my face. Not that it was the first time he'd seen me in a towel, but somehow after that kiss, something had changed.

He cleared his throat. "I was thinking I'd go check out the area while there's some light out."

I tucked the towel tighter under my arm and nodded. "I'm going with you. Maybe there are other survivors around."

He crossed his arms against his chest. "I should go alone, just in case. We don't want a repeat of our run-in with those looters."

"No way. Someone needs to watch your back in case those nephilim show up again."

He twisted the doorknob around, chewing on his lower lip. "What are the chances I'll be able to talk you out of coming with me?"

"Slim to none, so you might as well give up now." I shot him a grin. "Now go make us breakfast so I can finish getting dressed."

"Yes, ma'am."

He turned heel, and I closed the door behind him, leaning against it. I waited for a second until my heartbeats returned to normal. This was Asher. The same guy I used to take baths with as a toddler. I couldn't let things be weird between us. He was the only family I had left, and I wouldn't risk what we had for anything.

I dropped the towel and pulled my black top over my head. It hung limply from my body. I ignored it and slipped on my jeans and sneakers. I'd only brought three outfits for the road so this was as good as I'd get.

I joined Asher and Duke in the kitchen. They both hovered around the counter, Ash sitting on a barstool and Duke begging for scraps. He offered me a can of fruit cocktail as I approached.

"Thanks."

He shoveled a spoonful of it in his own mouth, not meeting my gaze.

I shifted from one foot to the other. I really wanted to talk to him about last night, but I couldn't figure out how to bring it up.

He glanced up at me, the spoon sticking out of his mouth. "Are you sitting or what?"

I slid onto the barstool next to him and set the can on the table. This was stupid; I should just say what I wanted to say. This was Ash after all. I could talk to him about anything.

A strong gust of wind followed by a loud crash sent my heart racing, and all thoughts of romance vanished. I dropped the spoon and spun toward the backyard. The sheet that covered the sliding glass door blocked our view, but it sounded like a huge tree had fallen.

"Stay here." Asher's arm whipped across my chest, barring my forward motion.

I gritted my teeth but stayed put as he crept toward the back door. Two smaller windows were on either side of the wall providing a direct view of the yard. He inched toward one, keeping his back against the wall. He pushed the beige curtain aside and peered out.

"What is it?" I whisper-yelled.

"Electric pole. It toppled down a whole string of them like dominos. Damn angels."

I gulped. The angels had already succeeded in cutting most of our power. "What's the point of that?"

"Even if the power plants can get the generators back up and running, they'd have to rebuild the entire infrastructure this way."

My shoulders slumped against the counter. How were we ever going to beat them?

Ash clenched his fists and marched away from the window and into the bedroom. I hurried behind him. "What are you doing?"

He pulled the gun out and stuck it into the waistband of his pants. "I'm going out there, and I'm not coming back until I find more humans."

I shook my head back and forth as fear unfurled in my chest. I'd seen that look in his eyes before. He was so damned stubborn. "You're going to get yourself killed."

"No. I won't." He pushed by me and headed toward the front door.

I darted in front of him and blocked the entrance. "You're not going out now. They're obviously out there waiting."

"Why would they wait? If they wanted us, they could just come in and get us. There'd be nothing to stop them. We're powerless!"

He unlocked the deadbolt and grabbed the handle. I dug my heels into the ground, pushing all my weight against the door and narrowed my eyes at him. "Don't, Ash, please."

He pulled and the door swung open, sending me flying forward. I stretched my arms out to avoid smacking into the wall face first, but a strong arm wrapped around my waist before I could make contact. My shoulder blades brushed against a familiar chest, and my body relaxed against Asher's.

"I'm sorry," he muttered in my ear.

A faint meow snapped my attention to the front porch. A scruffy old tabby pranced in front of the open door, and my heart stopped. Before I could unravel myself from Ash's arms, Duke took off after the cat.

"Duke! No!"

I raced after him, taking the steps off the front porch two at a time. Ash shouted after me, but I didn't stop. I couldn't lose Duke. Not now.

I sped down the sidewalk with Ash running after me. Duke and the cat had a good half block lead, but I wasn't giving up. I pumped my arms back and forth, my breath coming hard and fast. "Duke! Stop!"

The flapping of ginormous wings exploded behind me, and my heart lodged in my throat. Ice crawled up my veins as terror seized me, slowing my pace. A gust of wind pushed me forward, and I splayed my arms out to stay on my feet. I twisted my head over my shoulder and froze. A pair of huge gray wings blotted out the dim sky above me. I couldn't make out the angel's face under the shadow of its immense wings, but I recognized its sleek gold body armor. He was nephilim.

I squeezed my eyes shut and said a silent prayer.

A body pummeled into me, sending me scrambling to the ground. My chin scraped the rough concrete, and I bit my tongue to keep from screaming. A hundred and seventy pounds of boy bore down on top of me, his familiar scent coating me in a protective shield.

I turned my head and caught a glance of emerald green eyes in my periphery. "Ash?"

Then he was gone.

The heavy weight flattening me to the ground vanished. The warmth cocooning my body disappeared.

The scrape of metal against asphalt rang out at my side as the gun crashed down to the earth along with my heart.

I pushed myself to my knees and searched the sky. My best friend hung limply from the clutches of a nephilim a few meters up. Huge wings flapped, taking them higher and higher.

"No!" I yelled. "Not him. Please, take me instead!" I screamed and screamed, but the monster didn't spare me a glance.

My chest tightened, invisible hands clutching my lungs. Tears blurred my vision as I stared slack-jawed and helpless as my best friend evaporated into the murky sky.

CHAPTER 6

Was it possible to die of a broken heart? I was convinced I was about to. My feet dragged me to the house, everything around me a blur. I wasn't even sure how I made it back. I inhaled and thick, stale air filled my lungs. It felt like a herd of elephants sat on my chest. Tiny needles stabbed my heart, piercing a million holes into my already failing organ. I slammed the door behind me, a part of me hoping the nephilim would hear it and come back for me.

I crumpled down to the floor and buried my head between my knees.

I lost them both.

My chest heaved and sobs wracked my entire body. My shoulders trembled as hot tears rolled down my cheeks. I cried for what felt like hours. I bawled for my best friend, for my dog, for my parents and for all the people I'd lost in the past year. I was tired of being strong.

I lowered my head to the floor, the cold tile like ice against my cheek. I curled into the fetal position, pulling my knees tight against my chest. I was done fighting. It was over. There was nothing left to live for.

~

A WARM TONGUE licked my face, and my eyes snapped open. Duke's big black nose nuzzled my cheek. I pushed myself off the floor and wrapped my tired arms around him. His fur tickled my nose as I buried my face against his huge head.

"Oh Duke, you crazy dog. Do you have any idea what you did?"

He sat on his haunches and whined.

"You didn't even catch that stupid cat, did you?"

He cocked his head to the side, his long pink tongue dangling out of his mouth.

"They took Ash, Duke. He's gone." Tears pricked at the corners of my eyes, but I kept them at bay. If I started crying again, I'd never stop.

He huffed and lowered his head to the floor. His big brown eyes looked up at me sadly.

I glanced around at the dark empty room, a mirror image of what I felt like inside. How was I going to survive alone?

Duke whined.

I sighed as I stared at my only remaining companion. "You must be hungry, huh?"

His ears perked up when I got to my feet. He followed me to the kitchen, his tail wagging. I poured the rest of the dog food into a bowl and set it on the floor along with another bowl of fresh water. At least the water was still running.

I blankly stared at the floor as Duke chomped away at his food. My brain was still hazy, my body numb. I couldn't give up though, not yet. My dog needed me. You'd think a hundred and twenty five pound German shepherd could take care of himself, but you'd be sorely mistaken. Duke's hunting skills were severely lacking.

I glanced up at the kitchen counter, and my heart constricted. Ash's half-eaten can of fruit cocktail sat on the granite countertop. My breath hitched, my lungs struggling to take in air. Ash saved me. If he hadn't jumped on top of me, I would've been the one in the nephilim's clutches, not him. Why'd he have to be so damn brave?

Now I was alone.

Duke whimpered and rubbed his head against my knee. "I know you're here, buddy. But you can't talk back so you're not quite as good company as Ash." I patted his head, and he stuck his nose back into his food.

There was one thing I was sure of; I wasn't going to survive alone. Ash had the right idea about searching the neighborhood for other humans. There had to be someone else still here. I couldn't be the only one left.

Images of the rifle-toting looters flashed across my mind's eye. I pushed them down into the dark depths. There had to be some *good* people left.

A gust of wind blew through the sheet covering the broken glass door, and I almost peed myself. *Get a grip, Liv. It's just the wind.* I tiptoed over to the door and reattached the tape that must have come off when Duke snuck back in. I put my ear against the frame.

How had I missed it? The relentless flapping of wings had stopped. It was silent outside.

I stared up at the darkening sky. The angels were gone.

For a brief moment, the weight in my chest lifted. Had they returned to their headquarters in the south? Is that where they took Ash? Adrenaline coursed through my veins. This was my chance. I had to go out there now and search for survivors.

I darted to the bedroom and grabbed my backpack. The crumpled sheets on the bed reminded me of Ash and our night together. The kiss. I swallowed down the lump in my throat before it choked me and hurried back to the kitchen. I filled my backpack with as many cans of food and bottled water it could hold.

"Duke, come!" I rushed to the door, the clicking of Duke's nails on the tile right behind me. I slowly pulled it open and peered outside. Dusk settled over the abandoned neighborhood, not even a cricket chirped.

I took a deep breath and stepped out onto the porch. What was the worst thing that could happen? I'd get kidnapped by an angel and sentenced to life as their servant? At least maybe I'd find Asher.

Something sleek and black on the sidewalk caught my eye. I ran down the steps and the familiar object took shape. My dad's gun. Asher had dropped it when the nephilim grabbed him. I threw the gun in my backpack and marched down the quiet street.

The sound of my pounding heart roared across my eardrums. *Just breathe.* I took a few more steps and hazarded a glance up at the sky. Still clear. Not an angel in sight. No wings flapping, nothing.

My shoulders relaxed, and I let my arms swing by my side as I walked. I switched my focus from the sky to the houses. I peered into each one as I passed, hoping to find any signs of life.

They all looked identical to the one we had found: broken windows, boarded up doors, dark and uninhabited. I walked around the entire block then doubled back around. An eerie silence blanketed the neighborhood. I almost missed the hum of wings.

The upscale community was huge, much larger than I'd imagined. After walking for over an hour, pitch black surrounded me. I had to go back. Even if there were humans around, no one would be out at this hour.

The night belonged to the vampires.

I slunk back to the house, ignoring the growing lump in my throat. Climbing into bed, I pulled the covers up to my neck. I rolled over and stared at the empty side of the mattress. Tears burned my eyes. I hugged the pillow next to me, a slight scent of Asher still remaining. It was almost like he was still there with me.

The following morning, I got up and repeated yesterday's

exercise. My only hope was finding people; it was the only way I'd survive.

Duke's nails clicked along the asphalt as we surveyed the quiet neighborhood yet again. Slits of light seeped through the thick clouds, providing a hint of warmth. I wrapped the light jacket tighter around myself, thanking Mother Nature for a relatively warm spring.

"Let's go another few blocks and then we'll turn back."

Duke barked and ran a few steps ahead of me. At least someone was enjoying the stroll.

A sharp whistle sent my heart racing. I yanked my gun out of my backpack, and I whipped my head from side to side to determine the direction of the sound. It stopped. *What the hell?* I took another step forward, and a long whistle followed by a short one carried through the air. It was coming from the house across the street.

I darted toward the pale yellow house, straining to hear something. A faint whistling started up again, and this time I recognized a tune. Yankee Doodle. Only a human would know that classic melody.

I rushed up the stairs to the large front porch. The windows and front door were all boarded shut. I put my ear to the door and could still make out the tune.

"Hello?" I whispered. "Is anyone in there?"

Slow footsteps drew near the door. I held my breath, one hand on my gun.

"Are you alone?" a gravelly voice spoke through the door.

I froze. Should I really answer that? "Yes," I finally said.

"Go around back. There's a window by the trash bins. I'll meet you there."

I grabbed Duke by the collar and tugged him around to the back of the house. Overgrown shrubbery crawled up the sides of the faded yellow walls, the grass almost coming up to my knees. Every window was covered in decaying plywood. I rounded the corner, and two large trash bins leaned up against the pale siding. I pushed one to the side and found a large window, the tall grass concealing it from view. It was just like the one we had in our basement.

A face appeared through the glass, and I jumped back. Duke growled, his eyes trained on the figure.

"Sorry, didn't mean to frighten you."

The man unlatched the lock and pushed the window open. He eyed the gun in my hand and frowned. "You can come in if you like, but that's not welcome in my home."

I paused, my fingers clenching the handle. What if this guy was a crazed killer? Was I really just going to walk into his boarded up house unarmed? Then again, he was the first human I'd seen in months that seemed to want to help me.

He must have noticed my indecision because he cracked a smile. "My name's Parker. I swear I don't bite. Can you say the same about that dog?"

I patted Duke on the head and he sat beside me, his big tongue rolling out of his mouth. "Yeah. He's pretty harmless—unless threatened." I had enough sense to add in that last part.

"You can leave the gun behind the trash cans. No one will take it." He shrugged. "There's no one left."

I pried my fingers off the handle and wedged the gun between the side of the house and the overgrown grass, pulling a garbage bin on top of it. I took a step back and admired my work. No one would ever see it if they happened to walk by.

I crouched down and came level with the large window. He swung the glass open all the way and motioned for me to enter. I eyed the opening, making sure Duke would fit and slid down feet first.

CHAPTER 7

I landed on a long wooden bench that ran along the interior wall. It took a second for my eyes to focus in the dim lighting. I'd been right; it was a basement and it looked a lot like mine. Tall shelves lined two of the cinderblock walls filled with canned goods, bottled water and medical supplies. A single cot sat in the corner adjacent to another door.

"Welcome to my home," said the older man.

"Thanks," I muttered. Duke jumped down behind me, his nails scraping the concrete floor.

The man leaned up against a wooden beam in the middle of the room, and my gaze traveled down his leg. A black brace covered the majority of it, from his thigh down to his ankle.

He pushed his graying hair behind his ears and hobbled over to a chair. He ran his hand over his thigh and rubbed at the bandage. "I messed my leg up pretty good a few months ago. The hospitals were all overrun by then so I did what I could."

He motioned to the chair across the table from him. "Have a seat. Tell me your name at least." He put his elbow up on the table and scratched at his unkempt gray beard.

"I'm good standing." I crossed my arms over my chest, staying near the window. I was pretty sure I could take the guy if things went south. He had a broken leg and looked to be almost sixty, but I didn't want to risk getting too comfortable.

"And your name?" He looked up at me through hooded blue eyes.

"I'm Liv and that's Duke."

"Nice to meet you both." His brows furrowed as his gaze bounced from me to Duke and back. "What's a young girl like you doing out alone?"

A pang sliced through my chest. "I wasn't alone. I just lost my friend. A nephilim—" My throat tightened, and I didn't want to cry in front of a perfect stranger. I bit down on my lower lip to keep the tears from falling.

Parker glanced down at the floor as I fought to keep it together. "Those nephilim took every able-bodied man and woman in the county." A rueful smile stretched across his lips. "I guess that's why I'm still here."

"Did anyone get away?"

He nodded. "The majority of Fallsbrooke cleared out before the war ended. Word spread that the vampires were getting the north. Most were more afraid of them than the angels. And yet, it's been those nephilim capturing people left and right."

"So you haven't seen any stryx or vampires?" I couldn't help the chill that raced up my spine when I said the words.

"They go where people are—for the blood. That's the one benefit of living in a ghost town."

I moved toward the wooden beam and leaned on it. "What do you think the angels are doing with the people they snatch?"

"Rumors are that they're turning the young men into soldiers for their army. The women are kept as servants. I've heard they've built training grounds around their headquarters in Washington, D.C."

"You mean the tower that reaches all the way up to heaven?"

He chuckled. "That's what they say."

"Isn't that what the nephilim are for? Why do they need more soldiers?"

He ran his hands through his hair, pushing it behind his ears. "Your guess is as good as mine, but I'd assume it has something to do with the vampires."

My head spun. Asher was going to be turned into an angel warrior and pitted against vampires? I couldn't let that happen.

"Do you know where they keep the humans they capture?"

He drummed his fingers on the table, the old wood wobbling. "A buddy of mine in D.C. said they built military style barracks all around the tower. That's where they're all kept, except for the ones lucky enough to get chosen to serve the head angels in the tower."

I really hit the jackpot with this guy. "How do you know so much about them?"

He reached into his back pocket and pulled out a black leather wallet. He opened it and held it toward me. A golden badge and an ID stamped with bold black letters flashed across my vision. FBI.

My eyes widened.

"I'm retired now, but I had a lot of friends in D.C. when this whole thing went down. They kept me in the loop while they could."

"What happened to them?"

He shrugged, his lips twisting down. "I don't know."

My gaze veered toward the window, the muzzle of the gun peeking up over the windowsill. "Wait. If you were an FBI agent, why didn't you let me come in with my gun?"

A small smile pulled at his lips, wrinkling the corners. "Honey, I've spent my whole life around guns and gun-toting criminals. The way you held that thing made it plainly obvious that you had no business carrying one around."

Heat diffused up my neck, and I was sure my cheeks were bright red.

"This is a small space, and I didn't want to risk that gun going off and bullets ricocheting off these walls. A bum leg is bad enough; I don't think I'd survive a bullet wound."

I laughed, and the tension in my shoulders released. I walked over to the chair next to Parker and sat. "Thanks for letting me in. You didn't have to do that."

The lines around his deep-set eyes crinkled as he smiled. "No, I guess I didn't. But what kind of a federal agent would I be if I hadn't? I swore to serve and protect my country and its people. I may not be able to do much anymore, but this was something I could do."

There was something I could do too. I could go to Washington, D.C. and find Asher. If the roles were reversed, he'd do it in a second. He'd never leave me at the mercy of warrior nephilim. He proved that yesterday when he saved me.

I gritted my teeth. I was doing this. "Parker, what else do you know about the angels?"

He arched a gray brow. "I know a lot of stuff. Could you be more specific?"

I chewed on a hangnail, fiddling with my fingers. "How do you get into their headquarters?"

He sat up, his eyes widening. "Don't even think about it, girl. I've known trained men that have gone in and never come back out." He snapped his mouth shut, his jaw twitching.

"Trained men? Like the military?" As far as I knew the humans hadn't tried to fight back against the angels or the vampires since the beginning.

When the vampires first arrived, our military tried to fight them off. Then the angels came, and we knew we were screwed. The vampires needed blood to defeat the angels so nearly all humans within a fifty-mile radius of D.C. were wiped out.

"Don't worry about it. It doesn't matter anymore anyway." His gray brows knitted together as he ground his teeth.

There was something he wasn't telling me.

He ticked his head toward a shelf over the table. "There's plenty to eat if you're hungry. I even have this fondue thing to heat up canned food. Makes it somewhat edible."

"Thanks, but I'm okay for now." What I really wanted was more information. Somehow I knew this guy could give it to me.

He slowly stood and limped over to the bed on the opposite side of the room. Next to it was a narrow door, which I assumed was the bathroom. "I'm gonna lie down for a bit. My leg's acting up; there must be rain coming," he said over his shoulder. "Make yourself at home."

I nodded and watched him make the slow walk across the space. A small bedside table stood next to the bed with two picture frames. I couldn't make out the faces from here, but it was definitely a family. Who had he lost?

I exhaled a slow breath and leaned my elbows on the table. If I stayed in Fallsbrooke, I'd become just like Parker. A girl, all alone, huddled in my own bunker. If I went after Asher, I could die, or worse still, be forced into servitude as an angel's foot soldier or vampire's blood slave. But at least I'd be doing something.

And if I found Asher…

My breath caught in my throat. I couldn't think about it yet. I didn't think I'd survive the disappointment if I failed.

Muffled snores filled the quiet room, and I glanced over my shoulder at my new companion. His chest slowly rose and fell, a small smile stretched across his bearded face. Somehow I got the feeling he didn't usually sleep much.

THE COT PARKER offered me was just like the one in my basement. Uncomfortable. After a few hours of fitful sleep, I gave up. Parker was still snoring away so I slowly rose and grabbed a granola bar from my backpack. I munched on it quietly as I scanned the basement in the daylight.

Dark gray walls boxed us in with the one window the only source of light. I gulped down some water and got to my feet. Duke picked his head up off the floor as I passed him. I put my finger to my lips, and he settled back down. Something on the far shelf had caught my eye. I silently moved toward it, my eyes darting back and forth between the shelf and Parker's sleeping form.

A cardboard box with rolls of paper sticking out of it perched on the top shelf. Below it were more boxes, each brimming with manila-colored files. I moved closer, running my finger over the dusty archives. What was all this stuff?

I pulled out one of the folders and flipped through the yellowing pages. Red and black lettering blanketed the documents: Property of the Federal Government, Private and Confidential, FBI and other lettered organizations I wasn't familiar with. I slammed the file closed and tried to shove it back in the box, but a stack of photographs slipped out.

I dropped to my hands and knees. As I arranged the photographs into a pile, I couldn't help but glance at the images. Angels and vampires—together. From the look of the angels' magnificent wings, they had to be the leaders. After almost a year of war, we'd determined that their wing size was in direct correlation to their standing within the angelic hierarchy. Nephilim's wings were the smallest and still they were larger than your average twelve-year-old was tall.

I flipped through more pictures. These had to have been taken after the war. There was no way the two immortal races would be caught dead in a room together before that. So who was running surveillance on them? Who could have gotten close enough to snap those photos?

The big box on the top shelf was calling my name. My fingers itched to pull down those paper scrolls. I got to my tiptoes and stretched. My fingers latched onto one of the rolls and pulled it down. I unrolled it across the floor. A set of diagrams inked in dark blue stretched out before me. Blueprints?

I turned it around and around but couldn't make it out. I stood up and reached for another one, my fingers grazing the top of the box. I pushed up on my tiptoes a little more and lost my balance. I fell forward, my hands pulling files down with me.

Duke jumped up and yipped as the folders and papers all tumbled to the floor. *Crap*! The snoring stopped and Parker jolted upright, his blue eyes fixed on me.

"I'm sorry," I muttered. "I was just… um… looking for food and I knocked over some of your stuff."

His eyes narrowed, and he scratched at his beard. "I did tell you I was an FBI agent, right?"

I gulped and tugged at the hem of my shirt. I wished I could pull it over my head.

He slowly stood and limped over to the mess of papers on the floor. "Did you find what you were looking for?"

"I didn't mean to snoop, I swear. I just really need to find my friend, Ash. The angels have him, and if you know something that could help me, you have to tell me." My lower lip quivered. "Please."

He sighed and lowered himself onto the bench alongside the wall. "What do you want to know?"

CHAPTER 8

I stared at the blueprints splayed out across the floor with my jaw hung open. Parker had detailed schematics of all of downtown D.C., including the new angel tower, which sat smack dab in the center of the National Mall. It didn't actually reach heaven, but it did soar over three thousand feet into the sky.

"How did you get all of these?" I sat back on my butt.

"I told you; I had a lot of friends in Washington."

"What were they doing with these blueprints? Were they trying to take the angels down?"

A rueful chuckle escaped his lips. "They've been trying from the beginning. They never stopped."

I glanced down at the angel tower. The diagram didn't seem as complete as all the others. The bottom third was marked with doors and stairwells but the top portion was blank. "Why is this blueprint missing stuff?"

"Because not many humans have made it past the fiftieth floor of Arx."

"Arx?"

"It's what we nicknamed the tower. It's Latin for fortress. We always had code names at the agency."

The blueprint was covered in pencil marks. I turned the document to the side and leaned in close to read it. They were notes. Tidbits of information someone had collected about the various levels. Where the elevators were, how many guards, emergency exits, etc.

"So the FBI has a spy inside Arx?"

He scratched at his beard, and I could almost see the gears grinding in his head.

"I'm not going to tell anyone. I'm on your side—the human side, I mean."

He exhaled through clenched teeth. "Yes, we have a couple."

Hope blossomed in my chest. "So are they going to take the angels down?" An image of big burly military men dragging the angels out by their wings flashed through my mind.

"I wish it were that easy." He rubbed his hand down his bad leg. "Right now they're gathering intel, trying to find a weakness. So far, they've found none."

My shoulders slumped, the heaviness in my chest back. There had to be a way in there. It's not like I was deluded enough to think I could overthrow the angels; I just needed a way to get Asher out.

I grabbed the diagrams of the area surrounding the tower: the barracks where the humans were kept. That's where I needed to focus my attention.

"Liv, you can't seriously be considering going by yourself. There's no way you'd survive. You wouldn't be helping your friend by getting yourself captured."

I knew that. I wanted to say that at least we'd be together, but I realized how stupid that sounded. "I have to try. He'd do it for me."

Parker furrowed his unruly gray brows and grunted. "You're

not my kid, but if you were, I'd lock you up to keep you from going in there."

I eyed the window across the room. I could make it out before he stood up.

"Easy, wildcat." He held out his hands. "Like I said, you're not my kid so I can't say what you can or can't do. I can, however, strongly suggest that you don't risk your life for a foolish mission that has zero chances of succeeding."

I exhaled a long breath.

"I can also try to help you."

My eyes widened, my heart rate picking up. "You will?"

"I'd go with you if I could, but we all know I'd only hold you back." He grimaced as he repositioned his leg. "I have friends though, and I can get you in contact with them once you arrive in the city. They may have more intel by now. Their numbers are growing everyday."

He grabbed a scrap of paper off the floor and a pen from his pocket and scribbled a note. He folded it and handed it to me. "This is the address for my buddy, Linc. Just tell him Parker Donovan sent you." He motioned to the note clutched in my hand. "I told him to take good care of you."

My throat went dry, and I swallowed down the unexpected emotion. "Thank you," I choked out.

"I wish I could do more." He stood and hobbled over to the kitchenette. "Now how about some breakfast?"

I nodded and shoved the scrap of paper into my pocket.

"As I said before, you're welcome to stay here as long as you'd like."

"Thanks. I think I'll head out tomorrow. Is it okay if I spend the night here again? If not, I can go back to the house I was staying at."

He pulled two dishes out from a cabinet and placed them on the table. "Stay. It's been nice to have some company."

I smiled and started to collect all the diagrams scattered across the floor.

"Take as many as you need with you," he said over his shoulder. "I don't think I'll have much use for them anymore." He emptied the contents of a can into a small pot and lit a candle underneath it.

"Thanks." I sorted through the pile of documents and picked out the ones I'd thought I'd need and shoved them into my backpack. Tomorrow I'd head south and with any luck, in a few days, I'd find Asher.

CHAPTER 9

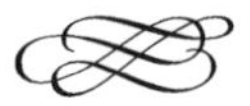

A sudden onslaught of emotions unfurled in my chest as the older man wrapped his arms around me. I'd only known Parker for two days, and yet the idea of saying goodbye to him killed me. He finally released me, and I took a step back. His eyes were shiny as I imagined my golden ones were. He'd gotten me through my first few days without Asher. I didn't think he'd ever know how much that meant to me. More than that, he'd given me hope. Hope that I might actually see Ash again.

"You better get going, girl." He ruffled my hair. "Remember what I told you: keep under cover of the woods, follow I-95 all the way down to D.C. and no fire at night."

I nodded, my teeth gnawing on my lower lip.

"You take good care of her, boy." He patted Duke's head, and he let out a whine.

I swung my backpack over my shoulder and hopped onto the bench to climb out the window.

"You sure you got everything you needed?"

"Yup." My backpack was filled to the brim with food and water, the rolled up blueprints sticking out the top.

"Good luck, Liv."

"Thanks for everything, Parker." I spun around before I could change my mind. I pulled myself through the window into the hazy morning light. Duke's head appeared in the opening, and I helped him out. I peered back at Parker through the glass one last time before picking up my gun and throwing it into my backpack.

I'd probably never see him again.

My vision blurred, but I swiped under my eyes, pushing the tears back. I had to be strong if I was going to survive this. And I would. I had to find Asher.

I followed Parker's instructions to get back to the highway behind the community. I didn't even need Duke to dig us a hole this time. There was an underground passageway that led me right into the cover of the woods.

I emerged under dense foliage with the highway to my left. I pulled the compass Parker had given me out of my pocket and followed it south. Washington, D.C. was three hundred miles away, which meant approximately one hundred hours of walking. My shoulders slumped, the mass of the backpack already weighing me down. Even if I walked ten hours a day, it would take me ten days to get there.

Maybe I was crazy to think I could pull this off.

I yanked on the straps of my backpack, pulling them tighter against my back. I could do this; I just had to stay strong. I patted Duke's head, and he rewarded me with a slobbery lick to the palm.

I hiked for hours, the crunch of leaves underfoot and Duke's panting lulling me into a daze. It was a good thing Asher and I had chosen late spring to embark on our journey. Or I guess it had been lucky that was when the food had run out.

I scanned the area as I walked, my eyes intent on the trees. If someone emerged from the highway, I'd see them coming a mile away. The woods were another story. The thick canopy of leaves blocked out the dim light from above, bathing the forest in endless murky shadows. I hadn't heard the flutter of wings since before meeting Parker. Maybe the angels really had gone south.

Duke wandered off to sniff a tree, something he only did when he had to pee so I let him, while keeping a close watch. I wiped the sweat off my forehead with the back of my hand and dug a bottle of water out of my pack. I took a few sips and put it up to my forehead. It was an old habit from when water used to be refrigerated. Now it was just barely cooler than my body temperature.

I lowered myself to the ground, my back against a tree. My calves burned and little blisters had already sprouted on my heels. If I could only rest for a few minutes, I'd quicken my pace to make up for it later. Duke trotted around the trees as I leaned my head back, a cool breeze rustling the leaves.

My eyelids drooped, my skull weighing a ton. I shook my head, chasing the sleepiness away. I had to keep walking while it was light out. Slowly rising to my feet, I whistled for Duke. He was at my side in a second, tail wagging.

"Let's keep going."

He barked and took off a few paces in front of me.

A big yawn escaped before I could stifle it. I smacked my cheeks with my palms to wake up. As I withdrew my hand, my gaze fell on the scar across my thumb. The angry red mark had faded a bit, a light pink jagged line remaining. It was a permanent reminder of the day the angels and vampires took their eternal battle to earth.

I'd been helping my mom chop carrots for dinner the night the news bulletin flashed across the TV. Vampires had invaded New York City. At first, we laughed, thinking it was some sort of joke. Then the videos started coming in. Thousands of humans died that night. It was stupid. I shouldn't have kept cutting those damn carrots, but it was the only thing grounding me as I watched in horror. My hand slipped, and the knife almost took my whole thumb off. I spent the first night of the attack at the hospital in Fallsbrooke getting my finger sewed back on.

When I came out of the surgery, I was so out of it, I thought the whole thing had been a terrible nightmare. I was wrong.

Mythical creatures had devoured a quarter of the population of New York City in one night.

Everyone had heard rumors of vampires' existence, but no one believed it. Not more than they believed in Big Foot or the Lock Ness Monster. Imagine the country's surprise when a fictional monster decimated one of the greatest cities in the world.

Then the angels came. For a while, we thought we were saved. Then things went from bad to worse. Humans were caught in the crossfire and before long we were left with this. Nothing.

The warring finally ended, but the majority of the country's infrastructure was destroyed, ecosystem ravaged, and human population near extinction. Those angels and vampires put us through hell. I hoped someday someone would send them back there.

Duke's ears perked up, and his head swiveled to the right. A low growl reverberated in his throat. I grabbed him by the collar and yanked him down to the ground next to me. I crept behind a tree and flattened myself against the rough bark.

The crunch of leaves carried through the quiet forest. Every hair on the back of my neck stood on end. The footfalls grew closer, my heartbeat accelerating with every step.

I stopped breathing, completely frozen as ice rushed my veins.

Two dark shadows sped by in a blur. They moved fast—inhumanly fast. They were at least twenty feet away, but I knew what they were. Vampires.

I remained motionless for what seemed like forever. Vampires had super-sensitive hearing and sight. I had to be sure they were gone before I emerged from my hiding spot.

I slowly stood, cursing every crackle under my foot. I peered around the tree into the dark woods ahead. Not that I could see much, but it seemed clear. I moved back to the edge of the forest within a few yards of the highway and continued on, my breaths gradually normalizing.

After a few more hours of trekking, I could barely see two feet in front of me anymore. Every last sliver of light had disappeared, and I was walking blind. I hated the thought, but I had to stop for the night. I glanced across the highway—still nothing. I hadn't come across a single house in miles. I dreaded the idea of spending the night out in the open, but what else could I do? At least it was warm enough that I wouldn't freeze.

"Duke, come here."

He turned around and cocked his head at me.

"It's bedtime."

I crouched down in front of a towering pine, arranging the leaves to make a small pillow and pushing all the twigs out of the way. I curled up into a ball, nestled underneath its thick limbs and Duke settled down beside me.

My body felt like it weighed a thousand pounds, my legs like jelly. Within seconds my eyelids drooped and darkness blanketed my vision.

CHAPTER 10

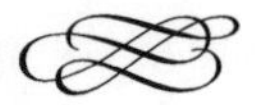

A rumbling engine echoed in my subconscious. It grew louder and more persistent until my weary body couldn't ignore it any longer.

My eyes fluttered open, goose bumps ravaging my skin. Fathomless black pupils locked onto mine.

I opened my mouth to scream, but no sound came out. Crimson streaks swirled through onyx irises, and my head spun along with it.

Duke barked, and the beautiful woman's gaze turned to him. She held out one finger, and he went silent.

She spun back to me. "That's a good girl," the woman purred. "Stay calm and don't move."

Flaming red locks cascaded down the vampire hybrid's shoulders. She crouched in front of me, cat-like in her stance. She was gorgeous and young, no more than a few years older than me.

Behind her, a dark-haired man lit a cigarette and popped it into his mouth. He looked bored. "Stop toying with her, Lissa," he hissed.

"I'm not. It's just been so long since I've seen a human in the wild." She ran her finger over my cheek, sending another wave of goose bumps over my skin. "She's still plump and pink. Not like the ones in the camp."

Did that stryx just call me fat? *Focus, Liv*. I squirmed back but hit the tree. Duke sat beside me, his eyes trailing the redhead.

"So drink from her or kill her. I want to get back to the den before some nephilim shows up." He flicked the ash from his cigarette and took a big puff.

"You're no fun, Felix. Besides the angels are gone." She inched closer, her breath icy against my heated skin.

My heart pounded against my ribcage, fight or flight fully kicking in. I wanted to run, but my legs were frozen. I'd heard about the vampires' compulsion, but this was the first time I'd witnessed it first hand. I had zero control over my body.

White gleaming fangs popped out from under the girl's pale lips. I gasped, adrenaline spiking through my veins. After all I had survived, I *so* did not plan on being sucked dry by a freakin' vampire hybrid. The pile of leaves and twigs I'd cleared the night before caught my eye. I splayed out my fingers behind my back and reached for the biggest branch I could find.

The stryx leaned in, her fangs inches from my neck. I jerked my hand up and jabbed the stick into her stomach.

She shrieked, her dark eyes popping open.

The compulsion cleared, and I jumped to my feet as she staggered back clutching at the branch sticking out of her belly. "Run, Duke!"

I got three strides in before two strong hands clamped down on my shoulders. There was a moment of pleasant weightlessness as I sailed through the air. Then my body slammed against a tree, knocking the wind right out of me. I crumpled down to the dirt, my head bouncing off the bark. Searing pain ripped up my spine. I sucked in a breath as my lungs screamed.

A dark shadow materialized over me, and I was sure I was dead. The man's fangs lengthened, and his lips twisted into a snarl. This was the end of Liv Graciene. I outlived my parents, maybe even my best friend and survived the immortal apocalypse only to be sucked dry by human-vampire hybrids.

The rumble of an engine reverberated across the quiet forest. *The same one from my dream?* The vampire spun toward the sound and behind him, a black motorcycle soared over the highway barrier. He leapt out of the way, releasing me just as the bike crashed down.

"Get on!"

My eyes bulged out as a guy in a helmet and black leather jacket held out his hand to me.

"Now!"

"But my dog—" I spun to the left and the right, but Duke was nowhere in sight. Maybe he'd actually listened to me when I told him to go.

The stranger grabbed my hand, his fingers closing around mine. "There's no time."

From my periphery, I could make out two black blurs heading straight for us. I gritted my teeth and jumped on the back of the motorcycle.

The guy revved the engine and took off. My body lurched backward, and I tightened my hold around the stranger's waist, my cheek pressed against his worn jacket. I squeezed my eyes shut as we flew through the woods, trees whipping past us.

The powerful engine purred underneath my legs as I did my best to hang on. I wanted to tell him to stop to force him to go back for Duke, but the words caught in my throat as we zipped through the forest, greens and browns blurring across my vision.

After a few minutes, he slowed and I hazarded a glance over my shoulder. The vampires were gone. I released the breath I'd been holding, and relaxed my grip around the guy's waist.

"Can you stop?" I shouted in his ear.

"What?"

The wind whooshed past, making it nearly impossible to hear.

"Stop!"

He slammed on the breaks and we skidded to a halt, barely missing the thick trunk of a monster tree. He pulled his helmet off, and jet-black wavy hair tumbled out.

"What's wrong?" His dark irises bored into mine. They were the most unique color I'd ever seen—a deep maroon.

"I have to go back for my dog."

He shook his head, unruly bangs sweeping over his forehead. "Are you crazy? You do know what those were back there, right?"

I unwrapped my arms from his waist and crossed them over my chest. "Of course I do; it was kind of hard to miss the fangs. I'm still not leaving Duke."

He huffed and jumped off the bike. It teetered for a second, and my arms shot out to my sides to keep from falling off. His hands were suddenly under my armpits, and he pulled me off the big bike. He smelled of pinecones and the air after a thunderstorm.

He lowered me to the ground and I staggered back, his maroon eyes intent on mine. His jaw twitched as he regarded me, a faint shadow of stubble lining his sharp angled face. He was the kind of guy all the girls at school would've been fawning over, if the end of the world hadn't happened. But it had. The attractiveness factor of this guy had no bearing in my life anymore.

I slapped my hands on my hips. "So can you take me back so I can find my dog?"

He mirrored my stance and shot me a snarky grin, revealing a sexy dimple. "No." He whirled back to his bike, which I now realized was a Harley.

I grabbed his arm and spun him toward me. "Are you serious right now?"

"Yes. Dead serious. I didn't risk my life to save your butt just so you could turn around and get killed."

"I didn't ask you to save me."

His eyes blazed, the maroon almost glowing. "Man, what was I thinking? I should've just left you there to get eaten by stryx. Not even a thank you." He raked his hand through his hair and mumbled under his breath.

A pang of guilt jabbed me in the gut. Maybe I was being a brat. He *had* saved my life after all. I chewed on my lower lip with my gaze to the ground. "Thank you," I muttered.

He turned around, his dark hair dangling over his eyes. "I'm sorry, I didn't hear that."

Wow, this guy was a royal ass. Here I was looking for some humans, and I get this guy? How was it possible that the one person that decided to save my life was a total jerk? "I said thanks for saving my life back there even though I didn't ask you to." Two could play this game.

He held his hand out and smirked. "I'm Declan by the way."

I eyed his hand and settled on a wave. "Liv."

"Okay, Liv. I'll make you a deal. We wait for an hour till the sun is out as far as it rises, and then I'll take you back. Even the stryx avoid the sun at its peak."

I paused for a moment to consider. Duke was smart; he'd be okay. With any luck, he'd run far away from there as soon as I'd yelled. Besides I was pretty sure neither stryx nor vampires ate dogs. At least I hoped not. "Fine," I finally mumbled.

Declan scanned the woods, his eyes intent on the shadowy depths to the west. He trudged over to his motorcycle and grabbed it by the handles. "Let's move closer to the highway. We can wait over there."

I nodded and followed him, the glint of the silver metal of his bike catching my eye. "How's your motorcycle still working?" I hadn't seen a functioning vehicle in months. The gasoline supply had run out halfway through the war and almost everyone had run out of reserves.

"It's solar-powered," he answered over his shoulder.

My head tilted up, and I stared at the murky sky. Even when the sun reached its peak, I didn't think it would be enough to power a vehicle. *Weird*.

We reached the cement barrier separating the tree line from I-95, and Declan leaned the Harley against a massive oak. He took off his jacket and sat down next to it. The tight black t-shirt he wore underneath clung to his sculpted chest, his biceps peeking through the short sleeves.

His eyes caught mine, and I dropped my gaze to the floor.

"Are you going to stand for the next hour?"

I wanted to say yes just to spite him, but if I was being honest, I was pretty tired. The few hours of sleep I'd gotten in the woods had hardly been enough. I moved to a tree across from him and slid down to the ground.

"You can sleep if you want. I'll keep watch."

"No. I'm fine." I straightened, pulling my shoulders back.

He regarded me with an amused smile, highlighting that cute dimple. "So what are you doing out here by yourself?"

"I'm heading south to D.C."

His eyes widened. "Why would you go there?"

"I'm looking for a friend." I wasn't giving him more than that.

"You're going all the way down there on foot?"

I shrugged. "If I have to." I eyed his motorcycle. "What are you doing by yourself?"

"I'm looking for someone too."

I guessed I wasn't the only untrusting one. He opened his mouth, but then snapped it shut as if he'd reconsidered.

"What?" I asked.

He huffed. "I'm headed south too."

Was that an invitation? "Um, okay."

Silence.

I picked up a twig and twirled it around my fingers. Maybe I should have taken him up on his offer to let me sleep. Now I didn't want to give him the satisfaction of asking.

"So this friend of yours, what are they doing in D.C.?" He barely looked at me as he spoke.

"He lives there." There was no way I was telling this guy about my crazy scheme. He'd probably leave me right here.

"Are you sure he's still there? The city's not what it used to be."

"You've been there?"

He slowly nodded. "I took off a month ago for the north."

"And now you're going back?"

"I'm not going back there. Ever. I'm headed to West Virginia." He closed his eyes and leaned back against the tree. "You shouldn't either."

CHAPTER 11

Declan didn't say another word until a half hour later. I was positive he'd fallen asleep, but how would he have known to wake up at the exact right time?

"You ready?" He stood, wiping the dirt off his jeans, his beefy frame towering over me.

I quickly jumped up and did the same. "Yup." I followed him to his motorcycle and hopped on behind him.

"Here." He turned around and handed me his helmet. "It's gonna be big on you, but better than nothing."

"What about you?"

He shrugged. "I don't really need it."

I considered for a moment and then pulled it over my head. I'd already seen how he'd driven through the forest. I couldn't imagine how fast he'd go on a deserted highway.

Declan pushed the start button and walked the motorcycle to a break in the cement partition. He revved the engine, and it roared to life. We sped down the highway, the wind whipping my top so it plastered to my skin. I was suddenly very grateful to be wearing a helmet.

Within minutes, we were back where I'd been attacked. The

ride had been much shorter this way. He slowed the bike to a halt, sidling up next to the barrier. An image of him flying over the cement structure as I was being attacked flashed across my vision. In all the commotion I'd completely forgotten. How the hell had he done that?

"Come on." He hopped over the partition like an Olympic hurdler.

I was not quite so graceful. I swung one leg and straddled the thing, slowly rolling over to the other side. When I landed, my eyes met Declan's. His lips were twisted into a half-smile.

"Are you mocking me?"

He laughed. "No, not at all. I just figured with those long legs, you'd be a little more agile."

My cheeks burned, and I cursed under my breath.

"So where is this mutt?" He narrowed his eyes as he searched the tree line.

"I don't know, and he's not a mutt. He's the only one I have left." I clenched my teeth as soon as the words slipped out of my mouth. Dammit. Where did that come from?

The weight of Declan's gaze bore down on me, but I refused to meet it. I knew what I would find there, and I didn't need his pity.

"Just help me find him, okay?" My voice sounded small and weak, and I hated it.

"What's his name again?"

"Duke."

I whistled and called out his name as we walked deeper into the woods. I tried to remember which way he had taken off, but it was all a blur of red hair and fangs.

"I never had a dog," Declan said, appearing by my side.

"You missed out. Duke's the best. He's my second German shepherd; they're great farm dogs."

Declan's penetrating gaze moved over me, and heat rushed through my veins. *What's that about*? "You grew up on a farm?" he asked.

I nodded. Damn, there I was spilling my guts again. Maybe it'd been too long since I'd been around other people.

"That must've been interesting."

"It was. Things were simple, uncomplicated. And it's probably why we survived for as long as we did."

"You and your family?"

"Umhmm. And my best friend." My chest tightened, my lungs inflating and deflating much too quickly.

"Your family's gone now?"

I slowly nodded, trying to catch my breath. The feelings I kept carefully buried bubbled up to the surface. "How about you?" I whispered.

"Dad's out of the picture, and I'm an only child. I thought my mom was gone too, but now I think I know where she is."

I glanced up at him and saw real emotions flash across his maroon eyes. Something dark lurked under the surface. Maybe I'd been too hard on this guy. "That's why you're going to West Virginia?"

"Yup." He dug his hands into his pockets and exhaled a long breath.

I called out for Duke again as we circled. He had to be nearby. He just had to be. "Duke!" I shouted again and my throat tightened, a lump growing.

"Duke!" Declan yelled. "Come on, dog. I got some yummy steak for you."

An unexpected laugh escaped my lips.

"What? Don't dogs love steak?"

"Yeah, they do, but if you had a steak, I'd probably wrestle Duke for it right about now."

He arched a dark brow. "You? Eat steak? You look more like a salad and veggies type girl."

My stomach rumbled. "Only shows how little you know me. They just don't make good steak out of a can."

"I'll give you that." He walked a few more steps and called out for Duke again.

I shouted for him, cupping my hands over my mouth. Nothing. I turned to Declan. "Maybe we should split up."

He shook his head. "Just because the sun's up doesn't mean the stryx aren't around for sure."

"Fine," I hissed through clenched teeth.

We'd circled the perimeter around the attack three times and still came up empty. I wrung my hands together to keep them steady. What if those vampires had gotten him?

"Duke, come on! Where are you?" I cried out. My throat was raspy from all the yelling.

Declan's head spun to the left. His brows furrowed as if he were concentrating on a particularly difficult math problem.

"What?"

"I think I heard something." His hand closed around my fingers, and he pulled me along with him. The unexpected contact made my stomach flip-flop.

According to my compass, we were heading south again. Maybe Duke had tried to track me after I'd jumped on Declan's bike. We trekked a few more yards, and he veered toward the west. "Do you hear that?"

I strained to listen. A barely audible whimper carried across the quiet woods. My heartbeat quickened. "It's Duke!" I'd know that sound anywhere.

I raced through the thicket, the whine getting louder with every stride. "Duke!" I yelled, and a familiar bark echoed back. I pumped my arms faster, my footfalls pounding the ground. My foot came down and shot out from under me as the ground abruptly fell away. I teetered over the edge for a split second, my heart lodged in my throat. An arm shot around my waist and jerked me backward before I plummeted down the steep decline.

I panted, my heart thrashing in my chest as warm arms encircled me.

“Are you okay?” Declan’s lips pressed behind my ear. A swarm of butterfly wings battered my insides, and it wasn’t the near fall that incited their mad fluttering.

“Yeah,” I choked out. He released his hold, and I spun around to face him. “Thanks. Again.”

Declan peered over my shoulder into the ravine I’d almost tumbled down. “I think we found Duke.”

CHAPTER 12

Duke's head popped over the ledge, and I yanked on his collar with both hands, pulling him over. His fur was matted with dirt and mud, but he seemed okay. He rewarded me with a big slobbery kiss as soon as he got to his feet, knocking me off my own. I wrapped my arms around his thick furry neck and squeezed. "Thank God you're okay."

Declan appeared next, his dark hair plastered to his forehead with sweat. He leapt over the ridge and pulled the rope up behind him.

There would've been no way I could have gotten Duke out of there without him. I didn't have a rope or the brute strength to push the dog out of the eight-foot crater. Declan had run all the way back to his motorcycle for the rope then jumped down into the hole like nothing.

I glanced up at him. "I guess I owe you another thanks."

"You just keep racking them up, don't you?" He coiled the rope up and swung it over his shoulder. "I'm sure I'll think of some way for you to repay me." He shot me a playful wink.

I rolled my eyes and started picking leaves and twigs out of

Duke's fur. "I wonder if there's a river nearby. He needs a bath bad, and I could definitely use some freshening up."

Declan sat beside me, brushing the fur and dirt off his shirt and swept his hair behind his ears. "No need to be so barbaric. There are some housing developments not far from the highway. I passed them on my way down; they looked pretty deserted."

"Okay, but we're going to have to walk. Duke can't exactly hop on your motorcycle."

Declan huffed. "This is exactly why I never had pets."

Just when I was starting to like the guy, he had to say something stupid. I stood and started walking back toward the interstate. "Listen, I appreciate your help and all, but no one said you had to come with us," I said over my shoulder.

Declan shot up, catching up to me in no time. "I could use a shower myself. I've been on the road for a while. Plus I'd hate for you and the dog to get eaten by some stryx after I busted my butt saving you both."

I suppressed a smile.

"Besides I have an idea on how we can get there faster."

I arched a brow. He smirked but didn't go into further details. We trudged the rest of the way back to the highway in comfortable silence.

The motorcycle was right where we left it, leaning up against the cement partition. Declan jumped over the barricade, and Duke and I followed him.

"Do you know how to drive one of these?" He straightened the motorcycle, holding it by the handgrip.

"I've driven a scooter, does that count?"

His lips twitched. "Close enough." He held out his hand and helped me on. "Give me your backpack. I can hook it onto the saddlebag on the back."

I reluctantly handed it over, nervous to part with my gun. "Wait, what about Duke?"

"You drive, and I'll carry him across my lap."

My eyes bugged out like a crazy cartoon character. "You can't be serious."

He shrugged. "You got any better ideas?"

I didn't. I straddled the seat and flicked the ignition on.

Declan's arms came around my back as he placed my hands on the grips. "This is the clutch." He twisted my wrist forward. "This is how to give it gas." He motioned to the opposite side. "And this is the brake. Also very important."

"Okay, okay, I got it."

Declan bent over and hauled Duke into his arms. "Geez, how much does this dog weigh?" he grumbled.

"About a hundred and twenty-five pounds but that was before. I'm sure he's lost weight over the past few months."

"Not much." He climbed onto the back of the motorcycle as Duke whined. "Hey I'm not enjoying this either, dog."

Duke's front and back legs dangled over either side of the bike as Declan's arm around his middle held him in place. Duke looked up at me, and I could've sworn he rolled his big brown eyes.

Declan's fingers closed around my hip, his thumb grazing my exposed skin. Heat ignited where our flesh touched, sending a rush of warmth through my body. That was unexpected.

"You ready?"

Declan's voice snapped me back to the present. "Yeah," I squeaked.

"Just take it nice and slow."

I revved the engine and lifted my feet, and we were off. My heartbeat accelerated as the bike picked up speed. Ten miles per hour, twenty, thirty. My palms were sweaty against the rubber grips, but I didn't dare let go to wipe them off. Adrenaline coursed through my veins, and the fear gradually melted away into excitement. This was way better than the scooter. I had to suppress the urge to rip the helmet off and feel the rush of wind through my hair.

"Take the next exit," Declan shouted in my ear.

I slowed down, switched lanes and cruised down the off ramp. The street looked like it had been a main boulevard at some time. Small restaurants lined both sides of the wide avenue, and a large shopping center sprawled to our right.

"That's it over there." Declan pointed straight ahead. A few blocks away, an apartment development sprung up off the main road.

I drove up to the abandoned guard gate and Declan lowered Duke to the ground, jumping off behind him.

"I think I'll walk the rest of the way," he said as he brushed fur off his shirt and jeans. His clothes were completely blanketed in black, silver and brown fur. "This is so gross."

"Sorry. I forgot to warn you about that."

"You better hope this place has hot running water." He pushed the gate up as I walked the Harley through.

"I'd settle for any type of water at this point."

We walked up to the first building and peered through the glass doors. The lobby remained intact, a sleek white desk lining the back wall. Modern white furniture completed the space giving it a clean and airy feel. It was the complete opposite of what I'd grown up with on the farm.

I pulled the handle, but the door didn't budge. "No wonder it's still so nice in there." Looters had gotten into a lot of buildings according to reports. I wondered how this one had managed to escape untouched.

"Here, let me try." Declan dug into his pocket and pulled out two thin pieces of metal. They looked like nail files but without the attached handle.

"What are you doing?"

"Watch and learn." He stuck one in the lock and then the other. He gave it a jiggle, and the door popped open.

My jaw dropped. "How'd you learn to do that?"

"How did you not? You can't expect to survive the apocalypse without figuring out how to jimmy a lock." He held the door open and motioned for me to enter. Duke snuck in first, and I followed right behind him.

To the right of the front desk was a long hallway; shiny elevator doors caught my eye. I pulled a flashlight out of my backpack and shined it down the dark hall. There had to be a stairwell nearby. I took the lead, my sneakers silent against the fancy marble floor.

"You know where you're going?" asked Declan. He'd been walking around the lobby, but apparently hadn't found whatever he was looking for.

"The stairs must be this way." I kept going down the darkening hallway until I came upon a door. "This is it."

We hurried up the first flight and emerged on the second floor. The door squeaked open, and Declan peered down both sides of the corridor. "Looks okay."

He pulled out his lock picks and got to work on the first apartment we found. Within seconds, the door clicked open.

"Geez, how many times have you done that?" He seemed like a pro.

He winked. "Don't worry about it."

The apartment was small, but nice. The style was similar to the lobby—white walls, modern furniture and high-end everything. Declan ran to the kitchen which was just off the entrance and twisted the faucet. Water dribbled down into the sink, breaking the silence.

"Yes!" I rushed over beside him to splash some on my face.

He kept his hand under the stream for a few minutes. "Damn, it's not hot though."

"I don't really care." I walked further into the apartment down another hallway. "I call first dibs on the shower," I said over my shoulder.

"Really? I'm covered in dog fur." He groaned.

I suppressed a laugh and continued to the door on the left. I pulled on the handle, and the door swung open into a bedroom. My eyes landed on the bed.

A scream tore out of my mouth.

CHAPTER 13

Declan was at my side before my mouth closed. "Are you okay?"

I nodded, but my eyes never left the gruesome scene on the bed.

He followed my sight line and grimaced, his nostrils flaring. He sucked in a breath and turned away.

Two bodies were splayed across the mattress, blood splattering every inch of it. Dark crimson painted the light gray walls. The stench of rotten garbage wafted up my nostrils, and I clapped my hand over my nose and mouth. Nausea clawed up my throat. I whirled around and raced out of the room.

I reached the kitchen and dunked my head under the cool water. *Please don't puke. Please don't puke.* I took a slow breath and braced myself over the sink.

A warm hand touched my back, and I jumped.

"Easy there. It's just me." Declan's breath tickled my ear as he came up behind me, warmth radiating through his t-shirt.

I swallowed hard, forcing the nausea back down and turned to face him. "Those poor people."

He pressed his lips together, his nostrils still flaring. "I should've checked the apartment. I'm sorry you had to see that."

I glanced up at Declan and noticed for the first time how calm he seemed. I hadn't seen my reflection, but I was pretty sure I looked like a hot mess. I could almost feel the green pallor settling over my skin. My brows knitted together. "You've seen dead bodies before." It was more a statement than a question. He was too composed, and there was no other explanation.

He cast his gaze toward the floor and nodded.

"Like that? All torn up?"

He leaned against the countertop and sighed. "Yeah."

I never wanted to again. I didn't think I'd ever be able to erase the grisly sight from my memory. "I can't stay here."

"We don't have to. I'll check the other apartments on this floor, and we can stay at another one."

I wasn't sure I wanted to stay anywhere near this place.

I took a step, and my head spun. I didn't know if it was the lack of food or gory scene, but I reeled back. Declan's arm snaked around my waist, and he led me out the door.

In the dark corridor, he leaned me up against the wall and pulled out his flashlight. "Stay here." He pointed at Duke. "You, dog, watch her."

Duke whined and sat at my feet. I watched Declan disappear into the next apartment and slid down to the carpeted floor to sit beside Duke, clutching my flashlight at my chest.

Alone now, the swanky building seemed much less appealing. Silence filled the air, making it thick and suffocating. I squeezed my eyes shut, and the horrible image of the couple flashed through my vision. I snapped them open and stared straight ahead into the darkness instead.

Duke nuzzled his head into my lap, and I scratched behind his big ears. If Declan hadn't found me in the woods, that would've been me. A chill raced up my spine, igniting goose bumps all over my body.

A door slammed, and I spun toward the sound, pointing my flashlight at it. Declan squinted and raised his hands in the air. "Just me. It's a no go on that one too."

More dead bodies? No wonder this building seemed untouched. The vampires must've taken out its entire population.

Twenty minutes later, Declan emerged from an apartment down the hall. "This one's clear."

I stood, not really wanting to stay in a building surrounded by dead bodies, but what other choice did I have? If I could at least get a good night's rest, Duke and I could head out on foot first thing in the morning.

Declan held the door open for me, and I peeked inside. "Are you sure there's no one here?"

"Yup. I'm pretty certain this was a model home. I don't think anyone ever lived here."

With all the ghosts crawling around this place, I wasn't so sure about that.

Pale light streamed in through the sliding glass doors so I tucked my flashlight back in my pack. I walked through the spacious living room and sat on the white leather couch. A vase was placed on the middle of the cocktail table and tall orchids spilled over the glass. I reached for a petal and rubbed the silk between my fingers. It was fake. He was probably right about the apartment.

"So that means no food, huh?" I glanced over at Declan who was searching the cabinets.

"Nope." He hopped up on the kitchen counter and checked the water. At least that worked. "I can go back to the other apartments. I'm sure I'll find something there. They're all open now anyway."

"Okay." I tucked my legs up into my chest, and Duke hopped up on the couch beside me.

"Why don't you go shower? It's the second door on the left down that hall." He pointed down a dark corridor. "By the time you're done, I'll have a full course meal ready." His lips twisted into a smirk.

"Um. Okay."

He left again, and I chased away the twinge of panic that sprang up in my chest. *Get it together, Liv.* I unfolded myself from the couch and padded over to the bathroom. Duke's nails clattered on the hardwood floor as he followed me down the hallway. I swear he had a sixth sense; he always appeared at my side when I needed him.

I turned on the flashlight and shined it across the bathroom before closing the door behind me. All clear.

The gurgle of rushing water soothed my frayed nerves as I stood under the immense showerhead. Even cold, it was one of the best things I'd experienced in weeks. The pitter-patter of the water drowned out the noise in my head and for five glorious minutes, I thought about absolutely nothing.

I toweled off and the tranquility faded, even the sight of my heart birthmark did nothing to quell my fears. Thousands of dark thoughts rushed back to the forefront of my mind. How was I going to survive a hike over hundreds of miles of vampire territory? I'd barely made it one night. Assuming by some miracle, I did, how would I get Asher out of Arx?

My chest tightened. Tiny fingers clasped around my lungs, squeezing hard. I gasped for air, dropping the towel. How was I going to do this?

Duke barked, and a light knock sounded at the door. "You okay in there?"

I inhaled a deep breath and picked the towel up from the floor. "Yeah. I'm fine. Sorry, I took so long. I'll be out in a second." I dried my hair off a bit more and pulled a clean shirt and my jeans back on. Staring at my haggard reflection, I sighed. Darkness haunted my golden eyes. There were some things that could never be unseen.

Declan lounged shirtless on a barstool at the marble island in the kitchen. Two plates filled with food sat in front of him.

I couldn't take my eyes off his perfectly sculpted bare chest. Until I saw the food. "What is all this?" I stared wide-eyed at the fancy spread. It was the first time I'd seen food that actually looked good in ages.

He held his hand out palm up and motioned to each item. "For your dining pleasure, madam, we have the finest Russian caviar atop water crackers as an appetizer. For the first course, we have pink salmon and cornichon pickles. And finally, the main course – filet mignon tips in a bourguignon sauce."

My stomach rumbled as my mouth filled with saliva. "What no dessert?"

"Don't ruin the surprise." He pulled out a bag of Milano cookies from under the counter and placed it in front of me.

A huge smile spread across my face. "I gotta admit it. I'm impressed." I jumped up on the stool next to him and dug in.

He took a bite and dropped a piece of meat on the floor for Duke. He devoured it in seconds then licked the tile too.

"I didn't even know they made all this fancy stuff in cans."

He shrugged. "Me neither, but thank heavens for it."

Heaven. I frowned and dropped my fork. *Stupid angels.*

He must have noticed my expression fall because he stopped eating and turned to me. "Sorry. I didn't mean to upset you."

"Nah. It's fine," I mumbled and shoved another forkful in my mouth.

His dark brows furrowed as he regarded me. "Was it the angels that got your family?"

"No. Vampires."

His lips twisted. "But I thought you said you'd never seen…"

"I didn't see it." Thank God. "My best friend found them. They'd gone out in search of food."

"The friend that you're going to D.C. to find?"

I nodded, not trusting myself to speak. I didn't want to get choked up in front of him.

"What's she like?"

"Huh?" I dropped my plastic fork.

"Your friend—the one you're looking for."

"Oh. He's a he actually. Asher." I swallowed down the thickness in my throat. "We grew up together, and he's pretty much the only family I have left."

He nodded and took a bite of the beef. "I'm sorry. I hope you find him."

My eyes cast down to my plate, and I blinked back the tears. Talking about Asher was too painful.

Declan's eyebrows pulled together, his jaw grinding. He clasped his hands together then released them. Finally, he looked up at me. "You can come south with me if you want. I won't go to Washington, but I can get you close."

The heavy weight that dragged me down since Ash had been captured suddenly lightened. "Really?"

"Yeah, it's no problem." He pierced me with his intense gaze. "Did you know that your irises sparkle like sunlight when you smile? They become the most vibrant gold I've ever seen."

Heat flushed my cheeks. "Um… thanks." I'd always thought their golden color was odd, but compared to Declan's enigmatic maroon, they didn't seem so strange after all.

He smiled. "Sorry if that was weird. I guess I just miss the sun." He shrugged and stabbed at a pickle on his plate and lowered his gaze.

Duke pawed at Declan and whined.

"Oh crap." My shoulders slumped. "I can't go with you. There's no way Duke can ride your motorcycle for hundreds of miles."

A small grin pulled at his lips. "I think I have a solution for that."

CHAPTER 14

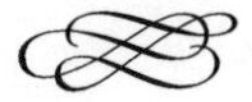

Hair tickled my nose. I opened my eyes to a furry butt in my face. "Ugh." I shoved Duke and rolled over. Somehow he'd managed to take up the entire king sized bed. I yawned and slowly stretched, feeling rested for the first time in days.

A yellow note on the bedside table caught my eye. I reached for it and read the scrawled message.

Went out for a bit. Be back soon.

~ Declan

P.S. You snore more than the dog does.

Whatever. I so did not snore.

I pushed the fluffy comforter back and scooted to the edge of the bed. A pile of pillows and blankets were strewn across the carpeted floor. I picked them up and threw them back on the bed. It had been pretty decent of Declan to sleep on the floor next to me. There was a spare bedroom with it's own massive bed that he could've enjoyed for himself. The idea of sleeping alone surrounded by corpses on all sides had been too much for me to handle, and he'd been sweet to offer.

Duke jumped off the bed and whined.

"I know, I know. You're hungry, right?"

He wagged his tail and ran to the kitchen. I'd have to take him outside eventually too, but luckily the dog had a bladder of steel. I poured out a big bowl of dog food Declan had found while scavenging last night and filled my own bowl with cereal. I munched on the crunchy oats as I flipped through an old magazine he must have left on the counter. It was the first one I'd seen in forever. It wasn't one of my favorite Hollywood gossip ones, but at this point I'd settle for anything.

Declan still hadn't told me what his plan was. How the heck was he going to get Duke on that Harley? Somehow I knew he'd figure it out. I'd only known him for two days, but he seemed pretty resourceful. I guess you had to be to survive this long.

Alone.

My mind wandered to Asher. Where was he? What were the angels doing to him? The only thing that got me through the day was the hope that he was still alive. He was young and strong; he'd make a perfect warrior for the angels. They'd be stupid to kill him. I clutched my arms to my chest. He had to be okay.

The front door opened, and I jumped. Maroon irises peeked out from under black hair. He swept his bangs to the side, and his eyes sparkled. "Come outside, I've got a surprise for you."

I tugged at the hem of my nightshirt which barely covered my butt. "Sure, just give me a sec." I walked backward down the hall toward the bedroom. I couldn't be sure, but I could've sworn I heard him chuckle as I left.

I threw on a pair of jeans and a sweatshirt over my nightshirt, not even bothering to change out of it and ran out to join him. "So what is it?" I sat on the couch and laced up my sneakers.

"If I told you, it wouldn't be a surprise now would it?"

I rolled my eyes and got to my feet. I called for Duke and the three of us emerged into the dark hallway. Declan flicked on the flashlight and led the way down the stairs. As we passed each apartment, I couldn't help but think of the mangled corpses inside. Whatever Declan had found, I just hoped it meant getting out of here as soon as possible.

We stepped out into the lobby, and my mouth dropped. Hitched onto the side of his motorcycle was a sidecar. It was old and rusty, the faded black paint in stark contrast to his sleek bike, but it looked big enough to hold Duke. I approached the funny looking thing and gawked. Inside the little rocket ship-shaped vehicle was a blanket and blue goggles. I pulled them out and twirled them around my finger. "What's this for?"

"I figured he'd need eye gear too."

I laughed, and my heart soared. This was really going to work. I was going to make it to D.C.

Before I could stop myself, I flung my arms around Declan's neck. He stiffened, his whole body going rigid. "Thank you," I whispered. His muscles relaxed after a beat, and he gave me an awkward pat on the back before I released him.

"Oh, I got this too." He bent down and revealed a pink helmet from behind the motorcycle.

I arched a brow. "Thanks. How'd you know it was my favorite color?" My voice dripped with sarcasm, and I hoped he got it.

"Hey, beggars can't be choosers."

"You managed to find a sidecar, but you couldn't find a normal-colored helmet?"

He shrugged. "Maybe I thought it'd be a good color on you."

I shook my head and smirked. "Come on, Duke, let's test it out."

We pushed the contraption outside, and Duke hopped on. I pulled the goggles over his head and adjusted them over his eyes. A hysterical laugh tumbled out of my mouth. This was priceless.

Declan jumped on the motorcycle, and I got on behind him after settling Duke in.

"Where did you find this thing? That's not something most people just have laying around."

"There was a bike shop not far from here. I guess I lucked out." He revved the engine.

"Thanks so much. I really mean it." The roar drowned out my words, but I was pretty sure he'd heard it. I wrapped my arms around his waist, and we were off.

We took it slow, driving up and down the main boulevard, but Duke loved it. His big tongue lolled out as the breeze rushed through his fur. After about twenty minutes, we headed back to the building of the dead.

I quickly packed up my belongings, anxious to get on the road. By motorcycle, the drive should only take about seven hours, even if we went slowly. I threw my backpack over my shoulder and met Declan in the kitchen. He was shoving cans and water into a reusable shopping bag.

"There should be plenty of space in the sidecar for this stuff."

"Great."

"We can divide the trip over two days so it's not too much. I don't know if you've ever spent seven hours on a motorcycle but it's not as fun as it sounds." He rubbed at his thighs.

"Okay, sure." I was anxious to get to D.C., but one more day wasn't going to change that much. I hoped.

He pulled a map out and laid it flat on the kitchen counter. He pointed at a spot in the middle of Pennsylvania. "We can shoot for around here as a stopping point. It's secluded and mostly farmland so I don't think we'll run into too many vamps."

I nodded. This was all him. I wasn't exactly an expert in reading maps or driving cross-country. I'd never left the state of New York.

He folded it up and shoved it in his pocket. "All right. Let's do this."

CHAPTER 15

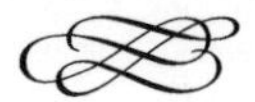

My cheek pressed against the smooth leather of Declan's jacket, dark hair whipping across my face from under the obnoxious pink helmet. I couldn't help but lean into his warm body, my arms tight around his waist. My shoulder blades burned, every muscle in my back tense from the hours on the motorcycle. I glanced over at Duke. His eyes were closed as he rested his head on the ledge of the sidecar. At least he seemed to be enjoying himself.

When Declan had suggested stopping halfway, I'd considered objecting. I wanted to drive straight through. Now I understood why. Every muscle in my body was screaming in protest. We'd only stopped once for a quick bathroom break about two hours ago, and I was so ready for another one.

I scanned the surrounding woods, nothing but tall green pines all around us. Declan had been right. Central Pennsylvania was pretty desolate; it reminded me a lot of back home. I bumped my helmet up against the back of his, and he craned his head back. "Do you think we can stop soon?" I shouted.

"Sure. I wanted to get as far as we could in the daylight. I'll get off on the next exit."

"Okay."

Daylight. That was a relative term. It was more like day*murk*. The murky cloud-filled sky never allowed real light to shine through. I'd hoped it would be different the further south we went, but there hadn't been much of a change so far.

Declan slowly turned off the exit ramp just like our whole ride had been—at a snail's pace. The downside of the sidecar was staying below fifty miles per hour. I couldn't complain though; anything was better than walking.

We hadn't passed a single vehicle along the highway with the exception of the broken down ones on the side of the road. Most had probably run out of gas as their owners had tried to escape. I still didn't understand how Declan's solar-powered motorcycle continued to run. I made a mental note to ask him more about it once we found a place to stay for the night.

Yellowing fields of corn stretched out on either side of the small road. One abandoned gas station sat off the highway and that was it. No restaurants, no supermarkets, nothing. This was definitely rural Pennsylvania.

Declan pulled up to an intersection and stopped.

"Now where?" I asked.

"Not sure. With all these corn fields, there must be farms nearby we just gotta find them."

I peered down a small side street, the pavement ending and giving way to a dirt road. "Let's go that way."

"You sure?" He eyed the gravelly road skeptically.

"Yeah. Most farms are off dirt roads. Ours was anyway."

He nodded and turned the motorcycle to the left, revving the engine. The pavement fell away, and the bike jerked along the rocky road. My teeth chattered as we bounced up and down.

After a few hundred yards, the unending fields parted, revealing a small red house with white shutters. A matching barn and silo stood a few feet away, both in the same dilapidated condition as the home.

Declan drove up the gravel driveway and cut off the engine. Duke hopped out of the sidecar and raced toward the nearest patch of yellow grass. I dragged my leg over the side of the motorcycle, my joints stiff and sore. I stood on the parched earth, my legs bowed like there was still a bike underneath me. I pulled off the helmet and reached to the sky stretching my arms out and inhaling a deep breath.

"How long have you been traveling this way?" I glanced up at Declan as his dark hair tumbled out of his helmet.

"Awhile now. Your body gets used to it."

We walked toward the door and up the steps to the small front porch. An old wooden rocker sat by the railing. We had one just like it. Dad used to sit and watch our old dog, King, and I run around the yard for hours after school when I was little. My throat tightened. I didn't have much time to think about my parents anymore. Besides it was better that I didn't. The pain of their loss was still too fresh. If I let it in, I'd never be able to keep going. And I had to.

"Let me go in first." Declan moved in front of me and jiggled the doorknob. The old wooden door creaked, the hinges whining as he tried to force it open.

"Why don't you just go get your lock pick?"

"Nah, I don't need it." He took a step back and kicked the door in. Splintered wood flew inside the house, the door coming right off its hinges.

My jaw dropped as I stared up at him. "Seriously?"

He shrugged. "It was old, and it felt great." He shot me a playful wink, revealing that cute dimple.

"Yeah, but now there's no door."

"It doesn't matter. Look around, the place is deserted."

I puckered my lips and frowned. I still didn't like it. Who knew what kind of wild animals came out around here at night?

Declan marched into the house, Duke and I trailing behind him. It was a quaint little home with wood paneled walls and flowery wallpaper. It reminded me of somewhere an old lady would live.

A large stone fireplace took up most of the sitting room, and I could almost picture my grandma sitting in her recliner in front of it. I shook my head, ridding my brain of the image. Thank God she'd passed before all of this started.

"I'm going to check out the back," said Declan as I headed toward the kitchen.

"Okay." I rifled through a few cabinets, finding the typical pantry items. After our stay at the fancy condo, we were pretty stocked up.

Declan's footsteps stopped, and the sound of a door clicking open echoed down the corridor. Duke growled, and the hair on my nape bristled.

A gunshot blasted across the silent space, and my heart leapt to my throat.

"Declan!" I raced toward the sound.

"Stay back, Liv. I'm okay," he shouted.

"Yeah, stay right where you are," another voice hissed.

I froze at the end of the hall. Declan's back was toward me, and a rifle pointing at his head poked out of a doorway.

"Please don't hurt him," I cried. The thought of losing my new traveling companion tied my stomach into a giant knot.

The man snarled. "Hurt him? You two are trespassing on *my* property."

"We thought it was abandoned." Declan's voice was remarkably calm.

I could hear the tremble in my own. I took a step toward them, the old wooden boards creaking under my feet.

"Hold it right there, young lady," the man said.

Declan's face turned to meet mine, and he gave me a reassuring smile. "Stay there, Liv. I'll handle this." He turned back to the gun-toting crazy guy, putting his hands up. "Like I said, we thought the place was abandoned. We were just looking for a place to spend the night. Put the rifle down." The words flowed from his lips like molasses, smooth and sweet.

The man lowered his weapon and poked his head out the door, peering down the hall at me. He had a full head of white hair and two missing front teeth. His lip curled into a half-smile when he saw me.

"Jesus, girl, what are you doing traveling on the road? You can't be more than sixteen."

I gritted my teeth to suppress the urge to yell at him. "I'm almost eighteen," I muttered.

"Out of the way, boy." He pushed Declan to the side and emerged from his hiding spot, throwing the rifle strap over his shoulder. "I thought you two were looters. There's been hordes of them making their way north." He trudged to the sitting room and sank into the recliner.

"We didn't see any on our way down." Declan sat on the edge of the couch, and I moved beside him, refusing to take my eyes off the squirrely old man. My knee bumped up against Declan's thigh as I scooted onto the sofa. The unexpected contact elicited a wave of calm over my frayed nerves, and my body relaxed. Why was I leaning into him? I shook my head and convinced myself it was a side effect of the shock of seeing him held at gunpoint.

"It's probably the vampires. The woods are crawling with them." The man eyed the busted down door and huffed. Then he reached for a jar on the side table and filled his mouth with some nasty brown stuff. "Where are you two headed?"

"Washington, D.C." The words slipped out of my mouth before I could stop them.

A surprised laugh lurched out of his mouth, stirring up a dry wheezing cough. "Are you crazy?" he choked out. "D.C. is completely overrun by them angels. You'd think they'd be better than the vampires, but they're not."

"I have a friend there. I have to go," I snapped.

"Suit yourself, girl." He spat into a cup, and I had to hold back the urge to vomit.

"Sir, could we stay the night?" Declan sure was laying the charm on thick. "If what you say is true about the vampires, I'd rather not go out in the dark in search of somewhere else to stay."

He frowned, chomping on the tobacco. After a pause, he pointed out the window. "You can stay out in the barn."

Jerk. I guessed it was better than nothing though.

"Fine. Thank you." Declan stood and I followed him, Duke right at my heels.

The old man dug into his pocket and produced an old keychain. He yanked one of the keys off and threw it at Declan. "You'll need this." He sat back in his chair. "I suggest you stay put till daybreak. And don't even think about lighting a fire or anything that might attract those monsters."

Declan nodded, and we marched toward the exit.

"And you better fix my door first thing in the morning. All the hammering would surely bring out the vamps at night."

"Yes, sir." He leaned the broken door against the doorframe, doing his best to cover the entryway.

Once we were outside, I let out a breath. "Geez, what an a-hole."

"Yeah, but let's look at the bright side—at least he didn't shoot me." He smirked, and I couldn't help but smile back. No matter how dire the circumstances, he somehow found a way to lighten the situation. I'd only known him a few days now, and yet it seemed like a lifetime. Maybe it was all the high-stress situations we'd found ourselves in since we met.

I couldn't help but think of Asher and compare the two. He was the only other boy I'd really gotten to know, and they couldn't have been more different. Losing Asher was the worst thing I could imagine, and somehow Declan made it bearable.

We trudged over to the barn, and Declan unlocked the big rusty padlock. He swung the chipped red doors open, and the scent of straw and manure assaulted my nose. *Bleh.* I held my breath and walked in.

"Hopefully it'll air out." He swung the doors back and forth.

I pulled my flashlight out of my backpack and shined the light over the large space. Four empty stalls lined the left wall; the rest was covered with hay and animal feed. And cobwebs—tons of cobwebs. A loft hung overhead filled with more hay, burlap sacks and a variety of old rusty tools. A mouse scurried out of a corner as my flashlight moved across the floor, and I jumped to the side, nearly climbing on top of Declan.

He laughed. "You know they're more scared of you than you are of them, right?"

"Whatever, they're gross." I extricated myself from his side and made my way toward a big pile of hay. After thoroughly checking for rodents underneath, I smoothed it out to create a makeshift bed.

Declan followed my lead, making his mound across from mine.

I lay my head on my backpack and yawned. All the exhaustion of the day suddenly hit me. "Goodnight, Declan." I rolled over and met dark eyes regarding me. One arm was splayed out between us, and I had the strangest urge to reach out and entwine my fingers in his.

His lips twitched, and he exhaled a long breath. "Night, Liv. Sweet dreams." His fingers brushed my arm, then slowly retreated.

Squeezing my eyes shut, I willed my racing pulse to slow. I needed to get my raging hormones under control ASAP.

Dark shadows danced overhead as the click-clack of critters scurrying about made my skin crawl. I wrapped my arms around myself, focusing on Duke's steady breathing beside me. In seconds, my lids drooped, and I fell into a fitful sleep.

CHAPTER 16

A hand clapped over my mouth and I jolted awake, my body bolting upright. My heart thundered against my ribcage as it made a frantic attempt to escape.

Declan's maroon eyes were wild and wide as he hovered over me. He pressed his index finger against his lips until I nodded in understand. He removed his hand from my mouth, and I drew in a quick breath.

"What's going on?" I mouthed.

"Vampires," he whispered.

I strained to hear, but I couldn't make out a thing. My lungs pumped hard and fast, and I willed them to slow their frenzied pace. My heart was pounding so loud I was sure the vampires all the way in New York could hear it.

The crackle of dry leaves made my heart stop. I froze, too scared to breathe. Eyeing my backpack, I considered grabbing my gun. Declan still didn't know I had one. I'd purposely decided to keep that from him until now. Not that a gun was going to do much against a vampire, but if it were stryx, it would at least slow them down.

"Don't move," mouthed Declan.

He must have read my mind.

The crash of splintering wood echoed through the quiet night. Footsteps stomped, and then a terrible cry rang out from the main house.

I gasped.

My legs trembled, my feet itching to run. I couldn't just sit here. They would come for us next.

Declan's warm fingers wrapped around my hand. "Breathe," he whispered. "You have to slow your heartbeats."

I nodded, my teeth clamping down on my lower lip. I took a long slow breath.

More footfalls. Approaching in our direction.

The rusted metal handle of the barn door jiggled. My eyes bulged out of my head, and I dug my nails into Declan's hand.

Duke growled, his hackles raised. I shushed him, but it was too late.

The doors crashed open, and Declan shot up to his feet. I lunged for the backpack and pulled out my gun.

Three vampires blocked the doorway, their tall lithe forms outlined by the moonlight. Blood dripped from their fangs, the bright red in sharp contrast to their freakishly pale skin.

I was wrong; vampires were ten times scarier than stryx.

The tallest one moved forward, and Declan yanked me behind his back. The vampire's black pupils were rimmed in crimson, an eerie glow emanating from the fathomless pits. He set his gaze on Declan, scanning him with an odd expression. The creature's dark brows knitted as he drew closer. The two males next to him waited, watching.

My hands shook, but I tightly clutched the gun. I'd never seen one used against a vampire, but at the moment it was all I had. Duke barked like crazy, growling and running back and forth in front of us.

"Brethren," he hissed, still staring at Declan.

"Get out of here." He glared through narrowed blazing eyes. "She's under my protection. I forbid you to harm her."

Okay, I was pretty sure Declan had lost it. What was he blathering on about? How was he going to protect me?

"Tsk, tsk," said the male, wagging a long finger. "By the terms of the Accords, humans on vampire territory are vampire property to do with as deemed fit."

"I didn't agree to those terms." He pressed me closer against his back. "You can take it up with Nathanael."

The monster's eyes glowed, fury flashing across his dark pupils. "Get out of our way or we will end you too."

"I'd like to see you try." Declan spun around and lifted me up over his head. "I'm sorry," he muttered, his maroon irises pulsating.

For a second, I was weightless, flying through the air. Then I landed on the loft above, flat on my stomach. *Oof*! All the air was expelled from my lungs. The clatter of my gun hitting the barn floor drew me to my hands and knees. I crawled to the edge and peered over the side.

Two enormous snowy wings sprouted from Declan's back and illuminated the entire space in an intense white glow.

My jaw dropped.

No. It wasn't possible. Declan was one of *them*?

I watched in shock as the three vampires lunged. Declan held his hand out, and a gleaming sword appeared in his palm. Blue flames danced across the long blade. He thrust his weapon into the chest of the tall vampire, and the monster screeched as the azure flames consumed him from the inside out. Seconds later, he was nothing but a pile of dust on the dirt floor.

Holy angels!

Duke barked, jumping up and down.

The remaining two pounced, each attacking from opposite sides. Declan swung his radiant sword in an arc, running the blade right across vampire number two's neck. His head fell off, hitting the ground with a *thunk* and rolling to the far corner.

My stomach roiled and nausea crept up my throat.

The last vampire jumped Declan from behind, wrapping his clawed fingers around his throat. Declan twisted and squirmed to shake the monster off, his large wings unfolding and flapping, but his grip was relentless. He swung his sword to the left then the right, but the vampire dodged each blow, staying just behind his wings and out of reach.

I clutched the wooden ledge, leaning further over the edge as they moved below the loft. Fear constricted my chest, its fingers tightening like a noose around my neck.

Declan's mouth gaped, his face growing redder by the minute. He released his sword, the glowing blade clattering to the floor, so he could use both hands to pry the vampire's fingers off his neck.

The vampire's fangs lengthened, and he chomped down on Declan's shoulder. A scream tore out of his mouth as blood and white light spurted from the wound.

What the hell? Or maybe heavens was more accurate in this case.

Declan's eyes rolled back as the monster sucked the life out of him.

No.

Adrenaline hemorrhaged through my veins. I couldn't just sit there and watch. Or could I? He was an angel. He was the enemy. My chest tightened as indecision clawed at my insides. I shook my head—*no.* No matter what Declan was, he'd saved my life. I owed him.

I leapt to my feet and scurried down the ladder, creeping behind Declan and the vampire. Duke was still barking and nipping at the creature's legs to no avail. A disgusting sucking sound filled the air as I crept forward. Holding my breath, I snatched Declan's sword off the floor and drove it into the vampire's back.

The vampire unclenched his jaw and shrieked as blue flames ignited in his torso. Working its way outward, the heavenly fire engulfed every terrible inch of him. Declan's eyes widened as they landed on me and then his sword, before he crumpled to the floor beside the mound of sooty ash.

I knelt down next to him, my heart racing. His eyes were closed and his wings had disappeared. I lowered my head to his bloodied chest, holding my breath. A faint thumping reverberated in my ear. I exhaled slowly, my shoulders relaxing.

He was still alive.

Could angels even die?

Blood trickled from the bite mark on his shoulder. I yanked my sweatshirt off and pressed it against the wound. Duke trotted over and licked his pale face, letting out a whimper.

"Declan, can you hear me? I need you to wake up." I hovered over him, willing him to be okay.

With everything that had happened, I hadn't had a second to process.

Declan was an angel.

I'd spent the last few days with one of *them*. None of it made sense. Why was he helping me?

Declan's breaths were slow but steady, his chest rising and falling in a rhythmic pattern. I lifted the wadded up sweatshirt from his shoulder, and my breath hitched. A golden glow emitted from the area around the wound. I pulled his shirt up to examine the bite more closely. The skin was healing right before my eyes. New cells replaced the old damaged ones, the flesh knitting together. Dried blood coated his skin, but the bite mark was barely visible anymore.

Unbelievable.

My fingers traced the area, his flesh warm under my fingertips. I let my gaze travel down his torso. His chest was well defined, his abs a perfect six pack. Besides the blood spatter, his skin was flawless. My cheeks flushed, and I pulled his shirt back down. I forced my gaze up, and his face seemed to have regained some of its color.

The adrenaline that throbbed through my veins just a few minutes ago faded, and each limb suddenly felt like it weighed a hundred pounds. I lay down next to Declan, propping my head on my hand, my eyes intent on his chest. *Please, don't die.*

A part of me felt like a traitor to human kind. I should've let the immortals kill themselves off and been happy. I shouldn't feel this way about the enemy. Guilt stabbed away at my chest as I watched Declan's sluggish breathing.

My lids grew heavy and no matter how hard I tried to keep them open, exhaustion finally won the battle.

CHAPTER 17

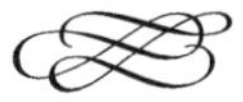

Light filtered in through the barn's skylight, and my eyes popped open. My arm was cold, the warm body lying next to it missing. I whipped my head from side to side, but Declan was gone.

"Duke?"

The barn door was ajar. I ran my hand over my face, pushing my messy hair back and plucking out a few strands of hay. I scrambled to my feet.

I peered through the open door, scanning the yellow fields. Duke galloped around the corner and barked, nearly scaring me to death.

"Geez, buddy. You almost gave me a heart attack." Obviously last night's assault hadn't had quite the same effect on him as it had on me. I patted him on the head, and he scampered off toward the main house.

The screams from the night before echoed in my eardrums. The old man. In all the commotion, I'd completely forgotten about him. I followed Duke toward the red house, which looked even more run down in the dim light of day. I stepped onto the porch, and the front door swung open.

Declan appeared, a rolled up carpet flung over his shoulder. My eyes widened as I scanned the lumpy bundle. He didn't say a word to me, just walked right by. Did he really think he could get away without talking to me about this? My eyes followed him as he trudged along leaving a trail of brown splotches on the dirt road.

I jogged up behind him, fully intending to give him a piece of my mind for lying to me all this time. As I neared, my stomach twisted, halting all the nasty words in my throat. Blood dripped down the edge of the carpet, splattering down his back and onto the ground. I gasped and froze on the spot.

Declan continued walking a few yards then dropped the heavy bundle on the ground behind the barn. He disappeared inside for a moment then reappeared carrying a long shovel. He plunged it into the dirt and began digging.

That poor man. I shook my head, chasing away the horrifying images racing through my mind. He wasn't the nicest person I'd ever met, but he certainly didn't deserve a death at the hands of those monsters.

Ice skittered through my veins. If Declan hadn't saved us again, that would've been me. I clenched my fists at my side as the fear melted, giving way to anger once again. Declan had lied to me this whole time. He couldn't just ignore me now.

I stomped over to the hole and glared at him, slapping my hands on my hips. "How could you not tell me you were an angel?"

He grunted and thrust the shovel back into the hard packed dirt.

"Declan!"

He glanced up, his teeth clenched. "I'm not," he hissed.

"What are you talking about? I saw your wings last night."

"I'm nephilim. I'm not a pure blooded angel." He lowered his gaze and continued digging.

"Same damn thing." I moved closer to him, my blood boiling. "You lied to me for days."

"Don't take it personally. I lie to everyone about it. It's not really something I'm proud of." A flash of regret crossed his dark irises.

"I don't understand. If you're nephilim, what are you doing out here? Shouldn't you be like manning their army or whatever?"

"I told you, I'm not one of them. Not in my mind anyway." He hopped into the hole, disappearing underground.

What the hell did that mean?

He leapt up over the edge a few seconds later, landing in a catlike crouch. My mouth gaped.

"So all this time you've been hiding your powers?" My mind flashed back to him carrying Duke out of the ravine. If he could jump out of this hole so easily, he could've done it back then too. Hell, he could have flown us to D.C.!

"I don't use them unless I absolutely have to." He dragged the body into the hole and began covering it in dirt.

My mind raced. Nephilim were half-angel and half-human which meant one of his parents was a pure angel and possibly responsible for the hell humanity has been through. But Declan had saved my life—a few times. Warring emotions swirled in my chest as I watched him bent over the grave.

"Why are you helping me? I thought angels and nephilim hated humans."

He looked up at me, dark curls hanging over his forehead. "They don't. Or at least they didn't used to." He swept his hair to the side and tucked it behind his ear, his forehead glistening. "And I helped you because those stryx were going to kill you. Both of our races have done enough damage."

"So you didn't take part in the war?"

He clenched his jaw and stopped. "Not after I realized how much damage we were causing."

I huffed.

He patted the mound of dirt with the shovel and tossed it to the ground. "The vampires are animals. I don't know how the angels could've reached a truce with them. It goes against everything I was raised to believe." He wiped his hands off on his jeans and leaned back against the old barn, staring up into the clouded sky. "It wasn't supposed to be like this."

"So can't you do something to stop them? You're one of them after all."

He slowly shook his head. "It's not that easy."

I crossed my arms against my chest. "You could at least try."

"I have." He shoved his hands into his pockets. "Leaving was my only option."

I suddenly remembered our earlier conversation. "That's why you're going to find your mom?"

He nodded. "My dad's an angel; he raised me. He told me she died when I was little. I discovered the truth during the war. He'd kept her hidden when the humans started dying." He shrugged. "I guess he still cared for her, somehow."

"What are you going to do when you find her?"

"I don't know. Just make sure she's okay I guess. I haven't seen her in ten years." He looked down, picking at some dirt in his nails.

"And your dad?"

"We're not speaking at the moment." The pinched expression on his face made it clear that was the end of that topic.

If his mom was human and his angel dad still had feelings for her, maybe she could convince him to stop all this destruction. It was a long shot, but at least there was hope.

"She won't be able to help you," he muttered and slid down to the ground.

I spun on him. "Can you read my mind or something?"

He smirked. "No, but after spending a few days with you, I've figured out how your mind works. Never play poker, you'd be awful."

"Thanks a lot." I kicked at the ground, sending up a cloud of dirt.

"It's not a bad thing to wear your emotions on your sleeve. It's better than not having any at all." His lips turned down, and his eyes dulled.

"What's wrong with the angels? Why aren't they protecting the humans?"

He shook his head, a dark look in his eye. "I don't know exactly. I'm pretty sure it has something to do with the vampires. Angels have always been stronger than those demons, but the ones that are here on earth are getting weaker. The vamps on the other hand seem to get stronger by the day. It's a very uneasy truce at the moment."

That didn't sound good. The last thing we needed was more fighting.

Now what? I still needed Declan's help to get to D.C. Without him, I was as good as dead. I couldn't trust him—not really. He was the enemy, but he was my only option at this point.

Duke trotted over, his big tongue hanging out of his mouth and he nuzzled into my leg. Then he walked over to Declan and lay down beside him, rolling onto his back for a belly rub.

A small smile pulled at Declan's lips. He ran his hand across his furry stomach, and Duke whined happily.

Duke always had an impeccable sense for reading people, and I trusted my dog with all my heart.

I walked over to Declan and slid down the barn wall to sit next to him.

He brushed his thigh against mine and turned to me, his maroon eyes like matching onyx pools. "I'm sorry I lied to you."

I nodded, a myriad of conflicting emotions swirling in my chest. "I guess you can make it up to me by getting us to D.C. safely."

"You still want to go there?"

"I have to."

He slowly inhaled, the early morning light catching his irises and setting them ablaze. "Okay. It's a deal."

CHAPTER 18

A neon green highway sign hung off the overpass holding on by a thin metal rod. Silver Spring, Maryland. Declan slowed and pulled the bike over onto the off ramp's shoulder. The border sign for Washington, D.C. loomed ahead in the distance.

He cut the engine and swiveled his head to face me. "This is as far as I go."

I knew it was coming. He'd warned me from the beginning he wouldn't go into the city, but still the surge of emotion was unexpected. My throat tightened, and I swallowed down a big gulp so I could speak. "Okay." That was the most I could muster.

I hopped off the big Harley and took off my helmet as unease filled my chest. "Come on, Duke, this is our stop."

My dog cocked his head at me and whined. I removed his goggles and strapped the leash on, pulling him out of the sidecar.

Declan pointed down the highway, refusing to meet my gaze. "Just stay along here, and you'll be there in a few miles."

"Right." I wrapped Duke's leash around my hand and clenched my fist. I could do this. This was the plan all along. I was going to Arx to find Asher and set him free. Alone.

"Keep an eye on the sky. The closer you get to the center, the more angels and nephilim you'll run into. Make sure you stay away from downtown. You don't want to be anywhere near the angel tower."

I weaved the leash in between my fingers, my gaze now refusing to meet his. If he only knew that was exactly where I was headed.

"Liv?"

"Hmm?" I glanced up, focusing on his black helmet instead of his questioning eyes.

"You're not going downtown, are you?"

I chewed on my lower lip. Damn, he was right; I did have a terrible poker face.

"Liv, you cannot under any circumstances go down there." He grabbed my arm and squeezed. "One of the nephilim guards will scoop you up in minutes."

"So? What does it matter to you anyway?" I wiggled out of his grasp, ignoring the tingles where our skin touched.

He grunted. "I didn't risk my butt saving your life multiple times just to let you do something stupid."

"It's not stupid. I have to save my friend." Hot tears stung my eyes, and my throat began to close. I willed the tears away, but my emotions got the best of me.

His eyes widened. Fire blazed in his irises, but his voice softened. "Save your friend from where?"

"The angel tower."

A string of curses flew out of his mouth. I didn't even think angels were allowed to use profanity. Then again, they probably weren't supposed to destroy the earth either.

"Are you out of your mind?" He threw his hands in the air. "No one gets out of that tower."

I ground my teeth together. "I have to at least try. Asher's the only person I have left in this world."

He shook his head, his dark brows creasing. "That's not true."

His words were so quiet, I wasn't even sure I heard him right. "You'll never get in. It's absolutely impenetrable."

I paused, debating whether to tell him about Parker and his friends. He was nephilim, technically one of them. I couldn't just tell him about the human resistance, even if he was half-human and claimed to be different.

"I can find a way." I pulled the blueprint of the tower from my backpack and unrolled it on the ground.

His eyes widened into maroon pits of darkness, and he jumped off the Harley. "Where did you get that?"

"It doesn't matter." I glanced up at him. "Have you ever been inside?"

He swallowed, his Adam's apple bobbing. "Yeah."

"Is it accurate?"

He examined the sketch more closely then let out a long breath. "Yes." He placed his hands on my shoulders and squeezed. "It's a suicide mission, Liv. You'll never make it out alive. What good will that do your friend?"

I squirmed out of his grasp, anger bubbling up in my chest. "Then help me!" I narrowed my eyes, shooting daggers. "You've been in there before. I might actually be able to get him out with your help."

I could almost see the gears grinding in his head as he struggled with the decision. A hint of hope flared inside me.

He gritted his teeth and hissed, "I can't go back there. I told you."

"Then leave me alone." I spun away from him and grabbed the diagram off the floor, shoving it into my backpack.

I didn't need him. I'd find Parker's friend, Linc, and we'd find a way to get Asher out. I marched back onto the highway, yanking Duke along with me.

"Wait," Declan growled and raced up behind me.

I didn't stop.

He yanked my arm and spun me around. I threw my hands up

to push him away, and it was like hitting a brick wall. His heated gaze captured mine and held me prisoner. For a moment, they were all I could see. He trapped my hands against his chest and warm lips smothered any lingering objection. My arms fell limp at my side as his tongue found its way into my mouth. Heat surged in my belly, rushing up my chest and racing to my extremities. A warm foggy haze settled over my brain as his hands roamed my body.

He suddenly pulled away, and my mind cleared. I sucked in a breath and pushed him back. "What the hell was that?"

He shrugged. "I was trying to distract you." He shot me a smirk. "I'd say it worked."

I rolled my eyes, running my hand through my disheveled hair and took quick breaths to mask the panting. My traitorous body didn't understand he was the enemy.

Declan's gaze locked on mine, his irises a smoldering maroon. "I'm coming with you—on one condition."

"What's that?" I arched a brow.

"We do this my way."

THE MOTORCYCLE RUMBLED to a stop in front of an old row house. The D.C. skyline rose up behind it, Arx towering over all the other monuments. The cold white structure was like a warning beacon in the darkening night.

I focused back in on the quaint home standing before us. Or at least it had been at one time. The windows were cracked, some boarded up and others left with sharp glass protruding. The colorful powder blue paint was peeling and covered in grime, dark red bricks crumbling off the façade.

"This is it." Declan pulled his helmet off and jumped off the bike, then helped me.

Duke leapt out of the sidecar to find the nearest patch of grass.

I stared up at the three-story home as Declan rolled the bike inside the formerly white picket fence. "Who lives here?"

"No one. Anymore." He jerked the kickstand up and scanned one of the gauges on his motorcycle. He turned to me, his expression odd. "Don't freak out, but I have to power up my bike."

"How? I thought you said it was solar-powered?"

"It is. Kind of." He raised his hands and white light shot out from his palms. My jaw dropped to the floor. The brilliant light streamed out until the dial on the gauge moved all the way to the green side.

"What was that?" I breathed out once he lowered his hands.

"Angel light. You've never seen it before?"

I shook my head. I'd never seen an angel or nephilim close up. I'd seen bursts of light in the sky while the fighting was going on, but I had no idea where it had come from.

I finally understood how Declan was one of the only people I'd seen with a functioning vehicle.

He climbed up the front steps and got to his tiptoes. Reaching up to the ornate ledge over the door, he produced a key. He stuck it into the lock and twisted, and the door swung open.

"How did you know?"

"Lucky guess."

Liar. It was a hard truth I'd learned, but Declan was full of secrets. I couldn't forget that. No matter how good of a kisser he was.

Declan led the way into the quiet house, the wooden floors squeaking with each of our steps. I flinched with every move.

"Don't worry," he said. "There aren't any humans within miles of here. They're all long gone, which means there shouldn't be any angels out looking for them."

The tension in my shoulders released, and I followed him into the living room. A worn-in couch lined the windowed wall, opposite a small brick fireplace.

He pointed at the staircase we'd just passed. "Bedrooms are

upstairs, bathrooms too. You should find running water—hot even. Angels like their creature comforts." He plopped down on the couch and stretched out.

I couldn't get his magical white light out of my mind. "What else can that light of yours do besides power a motorcycle?"

He pressed his lips together, covering his eyes with his forearm. "Lots of stuff," he muttered.

For someone who was usually so chatty, he'd gone weirdly uncommunicative. "Is that what's in your sword?"

"Yup. It's imbued with pure angel light, which is what kills the vamps."

"So why didn't you just flash them with your light?"

"I'm nephilim, only half-angel. I'm not as powerful. A full angel can take one down with a flash of the palm, but most use swords too. It takes less energy. Plus the longer the angels remain on earth, the weaker they become."

Hmm. Interesting. So they're not completely invulnerable.

Declan closed his eyes, and I could tell I wasn't getting any more information from him tonight. I trudged up the stairs wondering what had him in such a mood. At the landing, I opened the first door I came upon to my right.

Not the bathroom.

Light blue walls surrounded a cute little boy's room. A red racecar bed sat in the corner complete with blue and red racecar sheets. Toys were scattered across the floor as if whoever had lived there had left in a hurry. A picture frame atop a dresser caught my eye. I picked up the wooden frame, and a smile pulled at my lips at the image of the little happy family. A young dark-haired boy sat on the shoulders of a handsome tall blonde man with bright blue eyes while a brunette smiled a big toothy grin, her arm wrapped around the man's waist.

I looked more closely. There was something familiar about the little boy. The black wavy hair and those dark penetrating eyes.

"The bathroom is across the hall." Declan's quiet voice behind me made me jump.

I spun to face him, and his gaze fell on the picture frame in my hands. He swallowed hard and crossed his arms over his chest.

I was sure of it now. "This is you?"

He nodded, his jaw clenched.

"And your mom and dad?"

"Yup."

I scanned the room again and couldn't imagine a little Declan growing up here. "You grew up among humans?"

"Most nephilim do. Many of us don't even know what we are until we get older."

Mind. Blown. How could angels and nephilim have lived in our midst for so many years without anyone knowing?

"My dad didn't really live with us when I was young. He came and went. My friends all thought he was a traveling salesman." He walked into the room and slumped down on the bed. "I used to love this thing." He ran his hand over the bright red plastic.

There were so many questions I wanted to ask, but the look on Declan's face made it clear he wasn't in the talking mood. What had really happened with his parents?

He glanced up at me, his normally bubbly demeanor gone. His lips twisted down, and his hands fisted at his sides. "This was my childhood home, where I lived with my mom before she disappeared—before my dad told me she had died. We were just a normal family back then. After she left, he made us move out. Too many memories here, he'd said. And yet he kept the old house exactly how it was the day we left." He gripped the sides of the red racecar. "When the fighting started years later, he made me go with him to the angel tower, where I was trained to fight."

"Did you kill humans?"

His eyes refused to meet mine. It was all the answer I needed.

I spun around, the air suddenly suffocating in the small room. I needed to get outside.

Strong fingers wrapped around my arm, impeding my forward motion. I hadn't even heard him move. "Please, stop. Let me finish."

My eyes met his, and my chest tightened. The pain flashing across his maroon irises stabbed at my heart.

"I didn't do it for long. I refused. It wasn't right what they were doing to the humans. I told my father, but he wouldn't listen."

Anger blazed in my chest as I stared at the powerful creature before me. "Did you try to stop them?" He was strong like they were. He could've done something.

"I told you I tried." He shrugged. "It was too late. No one cared to listen."

"So you ran away?"

He nodded, his eyes cast down to the floor. "There was nothing else I could do."

A realization hit me, sending my heart racing. "Your father is *in* the angel tower."

"Yup."

"That's why you didn't want to come back here."

"Right-o." The tendons in his jaw flexed. "If he knows I'm here, he'll force me to go back."

Dread sprouted in my gut, spreading like a weed through my insides. How could I trust Declan? For all I knew, he could be leading me right into a trap. His father had to be pretty high up in the angel hierarchy if he resided in that tower.

"Then why'd you agree to help me?"

He shrugged, a small smile pulling at his lips. "You're a phenomenal kisser." His eyes sparkled, the playfulness returning.

I rolled my eyes but couldn't help the grin splitting my own lips. *Easy, Liv. He's still an angel no matter how hot he is*. "How can I trust you?"

"Because I saved your life. Twice."

"Yeah, yeah."

"And the idea of being the one to get a human out of angel

tower and spite my father and his generals makes me giddy." He winked, and the old Declan was back. "So what do you say? Are we still doing this?"

I was probably out of my mind, but I couldn't stop now. "Absolutely," I finally answered.

CHAPTER 19

A few dark curls tumbled over Declan's forehead, and I had to restrain myself from reaching out and sweeping them to the side. His eyes were closed, long legs stretched out and hanging over the edge of the red racecar bed. His lips were slightly parted as his chest slowly rose and fell, his entire expression peaceful.

How could he be one of them?

I still couldn't wrap my mind around it. He seemed so normal, so human.

I took a step further into his childhood bedroom and scanned the bright blue room. A bookshelf was filled with toy cars and motorcycles, only one shelf actually held books. I could almost picture the little boy in the photo on his hands and knees crawling around on the floor racing his cars.

I glanced at the grown version of the boy and moved closer to the bed. It was the first time I'd really gotten a chance to look at him without those piercing maroon eyes staring back. His silky black hair lay messily over his forehead and pillow. A light stubble dusted his jawline, surrounding pouty lips. The searing heat of his lips against mine flashed through my mind, igniting a swell of warmth in my middle.

I squashed those feelings down fast. Declan was just joking around; the kiss didn't mean anything to him. And it certainly didn't mean anything to me.

Liar, a voice in the back of my mind accused.

Even if it had, I had to focus on getting Asher back. That was all that mattered now. A pang of guilt sliced through my chest as I remembered the last night with my best friend. And that kiss.

My fingers ran over my lips as I remembered the way it felt. It was completely different from Declan's kiss—familiar, soft, and sweet. I shook my head, pushing the thoughts to the far depths of my mind. I couldn't focus on any of that right now.

"Penny for your thoughts." Declan's raspy voice tore me from my inner musings.

He stretched and pushed the covers back, revealing a bare torso and tight boxer briefs. A finely muscled chest and perfectly sculpted abs ran down the length of his body.

Okay, maybe he was too beautiful to be human.

Heat rushed up my cheeks, and I averted my eyes.

He chuckled and slid to the edge of the bed. "Have you been watching me sleep? Because if you were, I'd say that was kind of creepy."

I willed my cheeks to turn back to a normal shade and looked up to meet his sparkling eyes. "Just doing some recon on the enemy."

"And what did you determine?"

I shrugged nonchalantly. "You're pretty boring when you're asleep."

He shot me a mischievous grin. "Trust me, I'm anything but boring in bed."

I rolled my eyes, the fire returning to my cheeks. *Damn him.* I picked up his t-shirt from the floor and threw it at him. "Get dressed. I want to talk about the plan. While you were getting your beauty sleep, I was looking over the blueprints to find our best way in."

He tugged the shirt over his head, his dark hair spilling out. "I already told you, I'd handle it."

I'd been debating telling him about Parker's friend, Linc, all night. He could have information that would help us get Asher out, but I still didn't fully trust Declan.

"What?" he asked. "The vein on your forehead is jumping around like crazy."

I slapped my hand over my brow. No wonder he always knew what I was thinking. "Nothing."

"Just tell me."

Maybe I could tell him a half-truth. "You were wrong before when you said all the humans had evacuated D.C."

He stood and crossed his arms over his chest. "What do you mean?"

"I met someone when I was traveling, and he gave me a contact person who would help me." I fiddled with the hem of my shirt as I leaned against the bookcase. "I'd like to go see him."

"Because you still don't trust me," he growled and raked his hand through his hair.

"Can you really blame me?"

His expression softened. "I guess not." He grabbed his jeans off the floor and stepped into them. "I'll go with you to see him then. I'll tell you if his plan is better than mine or not."

I shook my head. "I can't bring an angel into their hideout."

His eyes darkened, his lips twisting.

"Even if I trust you, I can't betray them like that."

"Them? I thought you said it was just one guy?"

Stupid, stupid, Liv. "I don't know exactly."

He huffed, his biceps straining against his chest. "So you expect me to sit here and wait while you go out there by yourself?"

"Yes. Because trust goes both ways, right?" I fixed my eyes on his, steeling my gaze. "And I'd like to borrow your bike."

A big laugh burst from his mouth. "You're unbelievable, Liv." He paced in a small circle around his room. "How about a compromise?"

"What did you have in mind?"

"I'll take you as far as you think is safe, and I'll wait there. If you're not back in an hour, I go in after you." His maroon eyes blazed, they were practically glowing crimson.

"Fine."

DECLAN PARKED the Harley under the shade of a tall pine off the highway. He cut the engine and helped me off.

"You're sure you want to go alone?" He eyed me as I adjusted the straps on my backpack.

"Yeah. I'll be fine. It's not far from here." I clutched the map to my chest. If I was being honest with myself, I was slightly nervous. It was the first time I was going out truly alone. We'd left Duke back at Declan's house, and I missed my furry companion.

He held out his arm, flashing me his watch. "Let's synchronize our watches."

I suppressed a dramatic eye roll. "You're joking, right?"

"No. I'm not. You have one hour to see these mysterious friends of yours before I come after you."

"Okay, okay." I glanced at my watch. "Give me till noon." I handed him a folded piece of paper. "You have to swear not to look at this address until then, okay?"

"Right," he growled. "Because I might send a legion of angels to go flush out your friends."

I slapped my hands on my hips. "Look Declan, trust is earned, and so far you've been doing a pretty crappy job with all your lies."

He frowned and fiddled with his helmet strap. Then he shoved the folded note into his back pocket. "One hour, Liv. You better get moving."

I turned away, but his arm reached out before I got far, whirling me into his chest.

He pinned me with that merciless stare. "Be careful."

I licked my lips, my mouth suddenly dry. "I will."

I hurried down the path, refusing to turn back and look at Declan. I needed to for some inexplicable reason. As much as I wanted to deny it, he had gotten under my skin. Half-angel or not.

I stayed under cover of the trees for as long as possible before emerging onto the main road. According to the map, Linc's place was only two more blocks away. I moved quickly with one eye on the sky. The roads were deserted, not a single car or person anywhere. The sound of my thrumming heart was the only noise for miles. The street had been a commercial one, empty gas stations and strip malls lined either side. I expected a residential neighborhood, but I guessed Linc had chosen an unconventional hideout.

I reached the corner and made a left down Magnolia Avenue. The silence was thick, the thud of my sneakers on the pavement reverberating across my eardrums. I rubbed my sweaty palms against my jeans as I scanned both sides of the street.

A run-down ivory building with a wooden cross on the steeple caught my eye—630 Magnolia Avenue. The Church of Our Savior.

That can't be right.

I pulled the slip of paper from my pocket and double-checked. Parker's messy scribble might have been hard to read but there was no mistaking the number. This was it.

I walked up the steps to the simple wooden double doors. Each one was etched with a cross, just like the one over the building. I lifted my knuckle to the door and knocked, holding my breath.

Nothing.

I knocked again, a bit more forcefully this time.

I waited for a few more seconds and banged my fist on the door.

What if Declan had been right and there really weren't any humans left? Parker hadn't seen his friends in months—a lot could've happened in that time. My shoulders slumped, a mass in my chest weighing me down.

I backed away from the door, feeling like I was wearing lead shoes. I slouched down on the steps and buried my face in my hands. I had been so sure Linc would be the answer. How was I going to get Asher back now?

Trusting Declan was my only option left.

A faint creak on the other side of the door yanked me from my dark thoughts. I jumped up. "Hello? Is anyone there?"

A small slit slid open, and a pair of blue eyes appeared. "What do you want?"

CHAPTER 20

I ran up to the door, my breaths quickening. "I'm here to see Linc. Parker Donovan sent me."

The opening slammed shut.

"Hello?"

Footsteps shuffled away from the door, and my heart sank. I banged on the thick wood. "Please. Parker said Linc could help me. I need to get my friend out of Arx."

The shuffling stopped. I leaned in closer, whispering through the crack in the door. "Parker said you were his friend. He said you could get me in."

The slit in the door reappeared only this time dark green eyes peered through. "You know Parker?"

I nodded quickly. "He gave me this." I pulled the note and the blueprints out from my backpack and pushed them up against the hole.

His eyes widened. "Put that away before someone sees it," he hissed. "Angels have the keenest vision I've ever seen. They could be flying over us right now."

"Sorry." I shoved the diagram back in my pack. "So will you let me in?"

He grunted. "Wait five minutes then circle around back toward the left. There's a toolshed. The door's unlocked."

"Okay." I backed away from the door and hurried down the steps. I didn't like being out in the open like this, but what other choice did I have? I stared at my watch as the minutes ticked by. Only forty-five more minutes till Declan stormed in. I had to make this quick.

I counted down the last sixty seconds and raced around back. A dingy yellow toolshed stood at the back of the parking lot. A padlock held the two doors together, but it was unlocked. I pulled it out of the latch and slowly opened the door.

A stale musty odor swirled around me making my nose twitch. I fumbled around in the darkness until my eyes adjusted. A small window let in a few flickers of light, and I was finally able to scan the tight quarters. A variety of tools lined the wooden walls and a decent-sized ride-on lawnmower took up most of the space.

I took a step and stubbed my toe. *Ow*! Glancing down at the floor to find what I'd hit, I noticed a rusted metal handle. I crouched down and pulled, digging my heels into the floor. With a sharp creak, the wooden hatch opened, and I tumbled backward on my butt almost hitting the big lawnmower.

I stood up, brushing myself off and peered down the hatch. A beam of light nearly blinded me. I threw my arm over my eyes, squeezing them shut.

"Come on down. There's a ladder," said the same voice I'd heard through the door.

I slowly reopened my eyes, waiting for them to adjust to the dim lighting again. Once they did, I found the ladder and climbed down the narrow shaft.

I hit the ground with a thud, my sneakers sinking into the packed dirt. Four men surrounded me—two holding flashlights and two brandishing guns. They all had buzzed haircuts and a hard look in their eyes.

Damn it. I knew I should've taken my dad's gun out of my

backpack before coming in. Now it was out of reach hanging off my shoulder.

I raised my hands and tried to look as unintimidating as possible as I checked out my surroundings. Steel walls enclosed the claustrophobically small space. A narrow table and two chairs lined one wall and beyond it stretched a dark tunnel.

The guy with the green eyes spoke first. "How do we know you didn't just steal that stuff from Parker?"

"I didn't." I pulled out the hand-written note. A twinge of sadness unfurled in my chest as I read over his words before handing it over to green eyes. "He gave this to me and told me to come find Linc." I shrugged. "I can't really prove it other than to say he was the nicest guy I'd met in a really long time. He found me at a bad time and gave me food and shelter."

"That sure sounds like Donovan," said the blue-eyed guy.

An older man stepped forward and grabbed the note. He had a white goatee and wasn't as beefy as the rest of them. Scanning the writing, a half-smile crossed his lips. He held his hand out to me. "I'm Lincoln Donovan." He drew out the first part of his last name with a long southern drawl.

My eyes widened as I scrutinized his face. His smoky blue eyes did look familiar. They were kind just like Parker's. "Are you his brother?"

He gave me a smile. "Half-brother. And who are you?"

I finally clasped his outstretched hand and gave it a firm shake. "I'm Liv Graciene."

"My brother must have thought a lot of ya to give ya my name. My operation relies solely on our anonymity."

Operation? I didn't want to give my ignorance away so I kept quiet. "Like I said, he helped me out through a hard time."

"Linc, we gotta give her the test before you go any further," said blue eyes.

He sighed. "Very well. Jayse, you do it."

Green eyes pulled a pocketknife out of his jeans and approached me.

"Whoa there, buddy. What are you doing?" I took a step back, but the circle of men closed in around me.

"Relax," said Linc. "We have to make sure you're not one of them."

"It'll just sting for a second." Jayse's meaty fingers clasped around my forearm.

"What are you doing? Let me go!" I squirmed, but his hold was like a steal clamp around my arm. He pried my fisted hand loose and ran the blade over the tip of my index finger. *Ow*!

A tiny sliver of blood appeared, and I winced. *Dang that burned.* He held onto my finger for a few more minutes then released me.

"She's human," he declared.

I stuck my finger in my mouth and scowled.

"Sorry, darlin' but we can't have no vamps or angels in here," said Linc. "They've got that superhuman skin; cuts heal up in seconds."

I nodded, remembering Declan's miraculous healing after the vampires attacked. I glanced at my watch. Only twenty more minutes. If Declan showed up, we were both screwed.

It was time to get this show on the road. "So can you help me or not?"

"You're serious about going into Arx?" Green eyes asked.

"Please excuse Jayse's lack of manners. We don't often spend time with a lady. Introduce yourselves, boys." He motioned to blue eyes then green eyes. "This is my son, Jaxon and that there's Jayse."

The two burly men held out their hands and I shook each one, suppressing a yelp as their thick fingers squeezed. Obviously they hadn't shaken a lady's hand in awhile either.

"And I'm Britton," said the last one, who hadn't opened his mouth since I arrived. He'd been lurking near the entrance to the tunnel.

"Britt was in the Army with my boys. He doesn't talk much so don't take it personal."

I shot him a half-smile and glanced back at Linc. "So yes, I am serious about getting into Arx. My friend was taken by a nephilim a little over a week ago, and I'm pretty sure that's where he's being held."

"Pretty sure?" The lines around Linc's smoky blue eyes crinkled.

"He's young and strong and Parker said they capture humans to serve them as soldiers."

"Umhmm." He stroked his white goatee. "That is true."

"You know it's never been done before, right?" Jaxon stepped forward, cracking his knuckles. "No one has made it out of there alive."

"But Parker said you had spies inside. Couldn't they help?"

Linc's gaze bounced to each of his sons then back at me. "My brother did go flapping his mouth to ya about a lot of top secret info, now didn't he?"

"He trusted me." I crossed my arms over my chest. "He knew I'd try with or without his help, and he wanted me to survive."

Linc exhaled slowly, his brows furrowed. "I can't put my men in danger. What you're talking about is a suicide mission. And I won't risk my guys inside being exposed."

"I'll help her." The quiet one, Britton, stepped forward. He looked a few years younger than the other two, maybe in his mid-twenties.

"Are you sure, Britt?" asked Jayse.

He nodded and turned to me. "I can get you in. I can't promise much more than that."

"Thank you." I swallowed down the lump in my throat. The suspicious part of me wanted to ask why he wanted to help, but beggars couldn't be choosers. And if Parker trusted these guys then so would I.

The line between Linc's white brows deepened as he stroked

his goatee. He let out a huff and faced Britton. "If you tell me the day you're going in, I'll alert my guys inside. They'll do what they can to help without compromising their identities."

"Thanks, boss." Britt gave the old man a tight smile.

I checked my watch: seven minutes. I gasped. "I gotta run. My friend's waiting for me, and he's going to worry if I'm not back."

"Your friend?" Linc's eyes narrowed.

I hoped to God Britton wouldn't want to test Declan when he met him.

"Yeah, he'll be joining us on the mission. He's got some insider information too."

Linc revealed a walkie-talkie from his back pocket and handed it to me. "We're on channel five. This way you'll be able to communicate with Britt when everything's set up."

I took it and stuck it into my backpack. "How long do you think that'll take?"

"Give me twenty-four to forty-eight hours, and we'll be in touch."

"Thank you so much." I couldn't help myself, I wrapped my arms around the older man and his big body stiffened. I suddenly felt awkward and backed away slowly. "I really appreciate this."

I shook Britton's hand, looking into his big gray eyes. Sadness and loss tinged his smoky irises. I knew the expression well; I saw it in the mirror every day. "Thank you."

He nodded and squeezed my hand.

"Good luck, darlin'," said Linc as I climbed up the ladder.

I threw back the hatch and burst through the doors of the toolshed. Five minutes to twelve. If I knew Declan, he'd come racing around the corner any minute now, angel sword ablaze. I dashed down the block, trying to get as far away from the little old church as possible.

Linc and his sons might be a little weird, but they were attempting to defeat the angels, and I couldn't do anything to jeopardize that.

I sprinted around the corner, pumping my arms as fast as I could as my sneakers slapped against the cement. I didn't even bother to check the sky as I sped toward the highway.

I reached the woods flanking the interstate and could just make out Declan pacing in front of his motorcycle. I waved my arms in the air back and forth. "I'm back! I'm here!" I shouted.

"Stop yelling," he hissed as I neared. "Are you trying to lure all the angels right to us?"

I hunched over, bracing my hands on my knees and panted. That sprint had sucked all the air out of me. "Sorry," I rasped out. "I wanted to make sure you didn't come after me."

He kicked at the ground, and a cloud of dirt swirled in the air. A well-worn path circled the motorcycle.

"You didn't look at the address, did you?"

He ground his teeth together. "I said I wouldn't, right?" He checked his watch. "You had exactly thirty seconds before I did." He stuck out his lower lip and leaned up against the bike. "So how did it go?"

"Good. I got a big Army guy to come with us, and we may even have help on the inside."

He arched a dark brow. "On the inside, really? Who are these guys anyway?"

"I don't know," I answered, chewing on my lower lip, hoping I hadn't said too much. "Declan, I'm trusting you big time with this. These guys would go ballistic if they knew what you were." I squared off in front of him, fixing him with my steeliest glare. "You gotta swear that you're on our side."

"I already told you I was. I don't know how many more ways I can say it."

"Swear on your mother."

His brows drew together, his expression darkening. "I swear on my mother's life that I'm on your side, Liv. I'll do whatever I can to get your friend out of there."

CHAPTER 21

Twenty-four hours and still no word from Linc. I twisted the knob on the walkie-talkie, flicking through a few stations. Static filled the dead air.

I paced back and forth, peering through the window that faced onto the street. The enormous tower loomed over the deserted city, an ominous symbol of the angels' infinite power over us.

I was sick of being cooped up in this house. We were so close to Asher, and I couldn't do anything but sit here and wait. It wasn't fair. Who knew what they were doing to him right now?

My fingers curled into tight fists. "Ugh!"

"What's the matter, the mailman forgot your gossip magazine?" Declan clomped down the stairs and shot me a grin.

"I wish." I couldn't remember the last time I'd seen a mailman or a new gossip magazine. I stared out the window, my sights fixed on the white tower.

He came up behind me, his shoulder brushing my back and every nerve in my body perked up at his proximity. He pushed aside the worn curtain and followed my gaze. "Don't worry, we'll get there soon enough."

"What if we're too late?" Invisible fingers wrapped around my heart, clenching until its beats slowed to almost nothing.

"We won't be." He moved beside me and gave my hand a squeeze. "If your friend is strong and smart, they'd surely keep him. From what you've told me about him, he sounds like soldier material." He went to pull away, but I held on, threading his fingers between mine. Warmth seeped from his palm all the way up my arm, unfurling in my chest. The constant ache abated.

My entire body relaxed, the tension in my shoulders dissipating. The anxiety bubbling in my gut fizzled away. I hadn't felt so at peace since before all of this started.

I turned to face him. "Did you—?" A white glow emanating from our clasped hands caught my eye, cutting me off.

I jerked my hand out of his, and the light dimmed. A chill swept over me, leaving me cold and empty once again. "How did you do that?"

He shrugged. "All part of being nephilim."

"What did you do exactly? It felt incredible."

"Just a little angel healing power."

I wanted more of it. I wanted him to take away all my pain—to make it all stop. But how could I? I couldn't take advantage of his powers and still hate him for being an angel.

Maybe hate wasn't the right word. If I was being honest, there wasn't a single fiber in my being that hated Declan. It would be easier if I did.

The crackle of the radio yanked me from my inner ramblings. Declan and I both stared at the walkie-talkie as Linc's southern drawl came through in intermittent spurts.

"Ya there, Liv?"

I pressed the talk button, my heartbeats accelerating. "Yes. I'm here."

"We're good to go at twenty-three hundred hours. Britt will meet ya at the corner of Independence Ave. SW and 7th St. SW.

You'll go over the plan then. If you got any other questions, ask them now. I'm disabling this channel as soon as we're done."

My eyes widened and met Declan's. He shrugged.

"Nope, we're good," I finally answered. "We'll see him there. And Linc, thanks again."

"Good luck, darlin'. Over and out."

I dropped the walkie and wrung my hands together. This was it. We were going in there tonight.

"I hope these guys know what they're doing," huffed Declan as he walked away from the window and slumped down on the couch.

I followed, sitting beside him. "Me too." I clasped my hands together to keep them from shaking. My whole body felt like a blender, the insides churning like mad.

Declan reached over and covered my hands in his big one. "You gotta trust me in there, okay? No matter what."

I swallowed, my throat suddenly dry. "Okay."

"If anything goes wrong, I'll get you out of there." He squeezed my hands and warmth flooded my veins. "I won't let them hurt you."

I nodded, not trusting myself to speak. The roughness of his voice was doing things to my insides. An ethereal glow encompassed our hands and within seconds, my entire body felt lighter. I inhaled slowly and let the calm settle over me. He released my hand and leaned back against the leather cushions.

"Not that I don't appreciate it, but you can't be doing any of your angel tricks in front of Britt."

"I won't. Believe me, I've gotten pretty good at hiding what I am." He stretched and tilted his head back so he was staring at the ceiling. "I've been doing it since my powers emerged when I turned thirteen. It wasn't until all of this started that I was actually encouraged to use them. But after I saw the damage that we—that *I* could do, I stopped." He closed his eyes.

Not for the first time I wondered what he'd actually seen and done. How bad could it have been to make him abandon his father and his people? I squirmed on the couch, tucking my legs underneath me. When did everything get so complicated?

He turned toward me, his pupils dilated and the maroon blazing so bright it was more like a deep crimson. "I won't hesitate to use my powers and out myself if it means protecting you." His voice was thick with emotion, not its usual joking tone.

I nodded, the words stuck at the back of my throat.

"Rest up, Liv. It's going to be a long night."

LIGHT SNORING ROUSED me from one of the best naps I'd had in ages. I blinked and lifted my head from the puddle of drool I'd been resting in. On Declan's shirt. *Oops.*

We were still on the sofa. Declan's head leaned on the wall behind the couch, one arm draped over my shoulder. Somehow I'd ended up nuzzled in his chest. My heart stopped as I peered out the window into total darkness.

Son of a vampire! What time was it?

I shot straight up and stared at my watch. Just a little past ten o'clock. I let out a huge sigh of relief. Thank God we hadn't missed the meet up time.

Declan stirred beside me. "What time is it?"

"Time to get going."

"Ugh. Why is my shirt wet?" He tugged on the front of his blue shirt, which now had a large navy spot right above his right pec.

I pinched my lips together suppressing a laugh. "No idea."

He got up and stretched. "I'm going to give the Harley a little light boost." He held his hands palm up, and a pale yellow glow swirled around them.

Duke cocked his head as he watched the brilliant glimmer. It really was beautiful. I patted my pup on the head and went to the kitchen to set out a big bowl of food and water for him.

I couldn't bear the thought of what would happen if we didn't make it back. I found another two bowls in the cabinet and filled those too. "Just in case." I scratched behind his ears, and he let out a contented whine.

Declan appeared in the doorway, the moonlight outlining his broad silhouette. His dark hair tumbled over his forehead, drawing attention to his gleaming maroon eyes. He set his jaw, and a golden hilt appeared in his hand. Blue flames danced across the sword's glowing blade, beautiful and terrifying all at once. Every inch of him oozed strength and power, like an avenging angel sent down from heaven to save the world.

I couldn't take my eyes off him.

"You ready to do this?"

Adrenaline spiked through my veins and cleared the hot-angel haze. "Hells, yeah."

CHAPTER 22

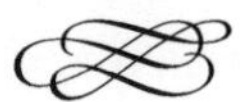

My jaw hung open as I stared up at the white behemoth stretching impossibly high into the sky and far beyond the clouds. No wonder people said it climbed all the way to heaven.

Declan put his finger under my jaw and snapped it shut. "You're going to let the flies in."

Yeah right. Like there were any bugs around. Even the insects had fled when the angels arrived.

The angel tower dwarfed all the surrounding memorials. Even the towering Washington Monument looked tiny in comparison to the ivory monolith. To the left of the colossal structure were dozens of gray Army-style barracks. A ten-foot barbed-wire fence surrounded the entire campus.

"Where is this guy?" asked Declan, his eyes taking turns scanning the sky and the dark streets around us.

I checked my watch. "He still has five minutes."

Declan had driven like a bat out of hell, getting us to the designated meet-up spot in minutes. Now the two of us stood on the corner of Independence Avenue, pacing the quiet angle. He'd hidden his angel sword at my request, and he seemed tense without it. I was fairly certain Britt would run away screaming if he saw Declan wield it. And we needed his inside guys.

I stared up at the opaque black sky for any trace of glowing wings. "How come there aren't any soldiers up there?"

"Angels are arrogant, Liv. They believe they've won and would never think some lowly humans would challenge their supremacy. Especially not in the sky."

Approaching footsteps pulled my attention down 7th Street. Britton marched down the road decked out in Army camo from head to toe. His gray eyes honed in on Declan as he neared. I didn't want him to get closer than necessary. Just because *I* hadn't figured out what Declan was, didn't mean Britt wouldn't.

I jumped in front of Declan while Britt was still a few paces away. "Thanks for coming."

He nodded and gave me a half-smile, his gaze still fixed on the nephilim behind me.

"This is Declan. Declan, Britton."

The two men gave each other tight-lipped nods.

"So what's your plan?" Declan didn't waste any time.

The burly Army guy ignored his question and turned to me. "Let's hope we can find your friend in the barracks. They're much easier to access than the tower. My guy will get us in at the west entrance. He'll distract the nephilim guard for as long as he can, but once we're in, we're on our own."

"Okay." Nervous energy strummed through my veins. If Britton hadn't been here, I would've considered asking Declan to shoot me up with some of that angel healing power.

"What's your friend's name?"

"Asher St. John."

He took out a slip of paper and pen and jotted it down, tucking it back in his pocket.

"Do you know how many guards are on duty?" Declan asked.

"Half a dozen guarding the barracks. Dozens more inside the tower. Let's just hope we won't have to go in there."

"Why are you doing this?" Declan shot Britt a narrowed glare.

I slapped my arm across my companion's stomach. I didn't need him pissing off our only help.

"No, it's fine. I should've been honest with you from the get go." He ran his hand over his dark buzzed hair. "My little brother's in there. I've been wanting an excuse to go in for weeks."

Maybe it was a good thing I'd brought Declan along. I wasn't half as devious as he was. I would've never thought to question Britt's motives.

"I'm sorry," he muttered.

My eyes met his and I suddenly realized why the pain in his gaze had resonated with me. We'd both lost everyone we cared about. "Don't be. I would've done the same thing."

Declan arched a brow at me, but I ignored him. Motives didn't matter now. We just needed to get in and get Asher out.

"How can we trust that you'll put Liv's friend first?" Declan's eyes shot daggers at the big guy. "What if you abandon us as soon as we get in?"

Again he ignored him and faced me. "I promised to help you find your friend and I will. Once we do, I'll get you guys out, but I'm not leaving without my brother."

"Fair enough."

Declan eyed me unconvinced, but it wasn't up to him. I was the one calling the shots.

"Let's just do this." Declan turned toward the tower, pulling a baseball cap out of his back pocket and positioning it over his unruly locks.

"Not that way," hissed Britton. "Follow me." He walked a few paces then stopped in front of a manhole. He crouched down and heaved the metal lid off, disappearing down the dark shaft.

I lowered my foot to the first rung of the ladder and carefully climbed down with Declan trailing just behind me. The stench of raw sewage assaulted my nose, and I suppressed the urge to gag as I made the slow descent. Reaching the last foothold, I hopped down and lukewarm water splashed my legs. *Eww.*

"This way." Britt pointed his flashlight down the dank passage and Declan and I followed.

The whoosh of rushing water muted our footsteps as we moved silently through the passageway. After a few minutes, the tunnel we were following abruptly came to a dead end.

"Now what?" asked Declan.

Britt moved his hands over the brick wall, stopping every once in awhile to give it a tap. His brows furrowed as he stepped a foot to the left and repeated the procedure.

"What the heck is he doing? Declan whispered in my ear.

I shrugged and pressed my finger to my lips. I flicked his hat too for good measure. He was so impatient.

"Ah-ha." Britt pulled a long file out of his pocket and stuck it in between two bricks. He gave it a yank, and the brick popped right out.

Declan's eyes widened, the maroon practically disappearing in all the white. I guess Mr.-Know-It-All-Angel didn't actually know it all.

Within a few minutes, he'd pulled out enough bricks for a full-sized adult to get through.

"We'll be directly under the barracks when we pass through here, so no talking—got it?"

We both nodded as Britt crawled through the opening in the wall. Once he was on the other side, he stuck his hand through the hole and helped me in. I climbed over the crumbling wall and focused my eyes. It looked like the sewage tunnels we were just in only more rundown.

At the end of the cavernous space was a metal door. Britt walked toward it and we followed, my breath coming in short spurts. This was it. We were at the barracks.

Britt walked straight up to the door and shined his flashlight into a small hole. He stepped back and waited. My pulse quickened, and I had to restrain my foot from tapping.

The click of the lock resounded across the vacant space, and my heart jumped to my throat. Declan's fingers closed around my hand and squeezed.

The door slowly opened, and a tall man appeared in a crisp white soldier's uniform. He had the same buzzed haircut as Britt and similar meaty physique. The new guy pressed his finger to his lips and ushered us through the doorway.

A trickle of sweat dripped down my back as I crept forward. My heart pounded so loud I was certain I'd wake the entire compound. The man led us through a narrow corridor and up a flight of stairs. He opened another door and we were back outside, the dark night casting ominous shadows across the silent complex.

Dozens of gray trailers stretched out before us, the metal siding glinting in the moonlight.

Britt patted the guy on the shoulder and handed him the slip of paper with Asher's name on it. The man stared at it for a second then pointed to one of the trailers about twenty yards from us.

My stomach flip-flopped as anxiety chewed on my insides.

Britton nodded and mouthed, "thank you." The man turned and disappeared into the maze of temporary housing.

Britton ticked his head in the direction the man had indicated, and we moved silently across the hard-packed earth. My heartbeat quickened with each step I took. I couldn't believe after everything I'd been through, I was finally going to see Asher.

Britton stopped at the front step of the gray structure and pointed at me. He silently crept up the stairs, and I followed. He opened the door and peered into the quiet dormitory, motioning for me to do the same. I took another step up and crossed the threshold, my mouth gone completely dry.

Black blanketed the room, and I strained to see anything

beyond my nose. Slowly, a dozen beds took shape, each with a sleeping figure curled on top of it. I scanned each one, searching for Asher's tall form and short blonde hair.

A few of the silhouettes fit the description. With most under blankets, it was difficult to tell without getting closer. I turned to Britt and shrugged. He ticked his head toward the rows of beds, motioning for me to go.

I tiptoed through the quiet snores, every squeak of my shoes close to giving me a heart attack. There were three blonde guys that could've been Asher. I made my way to the first, a silent prayer on my lips. Not him.

I moved to the next. The guy was too old.

One left at the far corner. I crept further, my heart thrashing against my ribs. The guy's head was turned away from me toward the wall. I leaned over his sleeping form, holding my breath. The man grunted and rolled over.

I froze.

Not Asher.

My lungs deflated, and my legs grew weak. I gritted my teeth and forced myself not to collapse on the spot. I turned back to Britt who was anxiously waiting at the door and shook my head.

He mouthed a curse word, and I echoed it in my head.

We were going into Arx.

CHAPTER 23

Declan pulled the blue baseball cap down lower over his forehead so that his maroon eyes barely peeked out from underneath the bill. I glanced up at him, but he refused to meet my gaze. I didn't have any super powers, and even I sensed the tension rolling off him in waves. I swallowed, my throat parched like the Sahara. Britt's uniformed friend walked behind the three of us, a gun trained at our backs as we crossed the threshold into Arx.

Harsh neon lights flooded the entrance as we passed the gauntlet of nephilim soldiers. Golden body armor gleamed across their broad chests and gilded swords hung at their hips. They were almost too beautiful to look at.

Declan kept his head down as we passed. If someone recognized him, we were screwed.

One of the nephilim locked eyes with Britt's guy and moved toward us. "Where are you taking these prisoners?"

"New recruits, they're scheduled for Augmentation."

Augmentation?

The towering blonde's light brows drew together. "At this hour?"

"We're running a bit behind schedule. Too many humans coming in."

The nephilim's bright blue eyes scanned us from head to toe. Sharp angles cut his face as if he'd been drawn that way. His porcelain skin practically glowed under the halogen lights. He nodded to the soldier and returned to his place by the door.

I released a quick breath as we moved further down the bright hall. Arx was nothing like I'd imagined it. I'd pictured it decadent and luxurious with gold-covered everything. Something one would find in a lavish medieval castle. Instead, it was the complete opposite. Clean white walls and sleek modern fixtures surrounded us. Everything was so white it was almost blinding.

In the light, I could finally make out Britt's friend's nametag. Redson was stamped across a silver badge in thick black letters. The light glinted across his close-cut hair, giving it an auburn tint. Ironic considering his name.

He led us through a grand atrium and stopped in front of a shiny elevator and pressed the up button. Seconds later, the doors slid open and the four of us slipped in.

I opened my mouth to speak, but Declan squeezed my hand so hard I was sure he'd broken a finger or two. He glanced up at the mirrored ceiling, and the camera trained right at us.

I quickly clenched my jaw shut and let my mind wander instead. What was augmentation and where was Redson really taking us? The one question I refused to focus on was the scariest one of all—what if Asher wasn't here? What if he was dead?

A thick lump clogged my throat, and tears pricked my eyes. I squeezed them shut, refusing to cry in front of these guys. I couldn't think like that. Asher had to be okay.

The elevator whizzed up to the twentieth floor, and the doors glided open. Redson led us down another bright white corridor and stopped in front of a door. Augmentation was stamped across the front in big ominous letters.

Well you wanted to know what it was, Liv…

Redson swiped his badge across the scanner, and the door clicked open. He led us into the large sterile space and shut the door behind him, motioning for us to sit. A row of plastic blue chairs lined the white wall. I sat and scanned the strange room. A desk was positioned directly across from us with what looked like a telescope sitting on top of it. Above the desk was another camera. A red light blinked as it watched us. Who was on the other end?

Redson flipped a switch by the doorframe, and the red light turned off.

"Okay, you're free to talk now." He moved toward Britt and took a seat beside him.

Declan eyed the camera overhead and ticked his head toward it.

"It's off," said Redson. "It interferes with the augmentation ray so this room is one of the only ones in the entire tower equipped with a shut-off switch."

What the heck is an augmentation ray?

Declan nodded. Apparently he knew what it was. More lies. My fingers curled into tight fists as I suppressed the urge to yell at him. I couldn't out him now.

"We're looking for Liv's friend." Britt turned to Redson. "His name's Asher like I showed you earlier. Any idea where he might be?"

Redson grunted. "Dude, we get hundreds of new recruits everyday. I can't keep track of them all."

My shoulders sagged against the hard chair. *Where are you, Asher?*

"You haven't seen my brother, Jesse, have you?"

"Naw, man. I'm sorry. I've been keeping an eye out too since I got word."

Was I the only one that wanted to know what the hell the augmentation ray was?

"Do you know when this guy was brought in?" Redson turned

to me.

"About a week ago." It seemed like a lifetime.

"He would've already undergone augmentation," muttered Declan.

Redson arched a brow, but didn't ask. "He's right. He would've been assigned a post by now. If he's not in the barracks, he must be on duty. Most likely levels one through five. That's where they assign the newbies."

"Okay, that's where we'll start," said Britt.

Redson chewed on his fingernail. "Unless they sent him out already. They sent a few hundred of 'em north a few days ago to keep the vamps in check."

Terror seized my heart. "Why would they send humans to do that?"

"They think we're expendable. Plus once they're augmented, they have more of a fighting chance."

I was pretty sure my head was going to explode. "What the hell does that mean?"

Redson pursed his lips and eyed Britt uncomfortably.

I spun at Declan who sat beside me still refusing to meet my eye. "What is augmentation?"

He ticked his head up at the shiny silver telescope sitting on the desk in front of us. "The angels found a way to infuse humans with some of their power. It's only temporary, but it makes them stronger, faster, and a bit more durable."

That didn't sound as horrible as I'd imagined. "That's not so bad. At least they're given an edge against the vampires."

"Yeah, except it screws with their minds," spat Britt, leaning forward on his seat so I could see him on the other side of Declan.

"How?"

"The more they get zapped, the weaker their mind gets." Redson stood and ran his finger over the telescope-looking thing. "It's a weird side effect. They start to forget the person they once were."

"It's too much power for the human vessel to sustain," Declan muttered under his breath.

All the air in my lungs evaporated. My head swam, and I grabbed onto the side of the chair to keep myself from tumbling off. Declan put his arm around my shoulder, but I shrugged him off. How could he not tell me?

I shot up from my seat, ignoring the spinning white room. "We have to find Asher now."

Declan stood beside me, his brows pinched. A flash of regret crossed his dark eyes. I knew he was sorry, but I didn't care. He turned to Redson and Britt. "If we split up, we'll cover more ground."

"This place is a maze, you won't be able to find your way out without me," said the burly soldier.

"It's not going to be a problem," Declan growled. Redson's gaze focused on him, and I thought I saw a flash of recognition.

"I have a blueprint," I blurted out. The last thing I needed right now was Redson outing Declan as an angel. I pulled it from my backpack and unrolled it in front of him.

The soldier scrutinized the blue ink for a moment and nodded. "Okay, it looks good." He pointed at level one. "Human guards are stationed here and here on each floor. There shouldn't be too many other angels wandering around at this time of night. If your friend isn't in the barracks and wasn't sent out to fight, he'd be on one of these other floors."

Britt gave me a tight-lipped smile. "We'll take the top two floors and you guys take the next two and we'll meet back on level one. Try to avoid the cameras as much as possible."

"Okay," I muttered.

Redson flicked the switch, reactivating the camera and opened the door. He walked us to the elevator and jabbed his finger at the call button. The first elevator arrived, and he ticked his head. "Good luck."

CHAPTER 24

Declan and I slipped into the elevator. The minute the doors glided closed, he threw his hand up toward the camera in the corner. A bright flash of light burst from his palm, and the intense flare momentarily blinded me. I squeezed my eyes shut as stars danced across my vision.

When I reopened them, a golden armor-clad nephilim stood in front of me. I almost screamed. Then Declan's maroon irises pierced me with their trademark smolder. My eyes widened as they raked over him in all his gilded angel glory.

"What the—"

He turned us away from the camera and pressed a finger to his lips. I reluctantly gave him a nod. How did he not tell me he could magically transform like that? One second he was in a t-shirt and jeans and the next he was in full warrior gear. He moved beside me and grabbed my upper arm.

I guessed I was supposed to be his prisoner or something.

I couldn't help my eyes wandering over his exposed arms. The nephilim soldier get-up didn't leave much to the imagination. The golden breastplate barely covered his chest, and his muscled thighs peeked out from under short leather breeches. His angel sword hung from his hip encased in a gold sheath, glistening under the neon lights.

The elevator doors slid open on level three, and Declan took the lead. The foyer split in two with a pair of human soldiers on each side. I quickly scanned their faces—not Asher. Declan took the corridor to the left, still clutching my arm. We passed under the narrowed glare of the two human sentinels, their uniforms an unearthly shade of white. Why were they looking at me like that? Like I was the enemy?

We circled the entire floor, passing a handful of other soldiers, but none were my best friend. On the bright side, we hadn't seen any angels either. Hundreds of questions swirled in my mind as we passed countless white doors. What went on in this place? Declan had to know; he'd lived here. He knew their secrets. I glanced at his hand clutching my arm. His fingers felt cold, completely different than the person I'd spent the last few days with.

We ended up back at the elevator and under the scrutinizing gaze of the human guards. Declan's foot tapped on the floor as we waited for the doors to open.

"What are you doing with the prisoner?"

Declan spun around and marched straight up to the guard. He towered over him, and the guy wasn't short either. "Are you questioning me, soldier?" he hissed.

The other guard standing next to the one who had spoken, elbowed his companion. "We're sorry, sir. He didn't mean any disrespect. It's just odd to see a prisoner escorted around the tower at this hour of night."

"Get back to your places and mind your own business," Declan growled.

The elevator dinged, and I darted inside and away from their questioning glares. These guys were worse than the angels.

And Declan was scary as hell.

I glanced up at the person I thought I knew, but in reality

couldn't have been further from the truth. The tendons in his jaw were clenched so tight, I could see them twitching.

His gaze met mine, and his expression softened. "I'm sorry," he mouthed.

The elevator stopped, providing me with the excuse to look away. I couldn't deal with any of this right now. I just had to find Asher.

More human guards greeted us at the second floor foyer, but no one dared question my angel escort this time. His dark brows were furrowed, his eyes blazing. He looked terrifying—in a glorious way.

Our footsteps echoed down the silent corridor as we passed door after door. What the heck did they keep in these rooms anyway?

We turned a corner and two armored nephilim headed straight for us. My breath hitched, and I lowered my head. They were both tall and broad chested with blonde shoulder-length glossy hair that any girl would kill for. Or kill to be with. Like all the angels I'd encountered so far, their cruelty was only surpassed by their beauty.

"Don't say a word," Declan whispered, shielding his mouth with one hand and the other tightening around my arm.

I kept my gaze cast down to the white floor, the tiny gray specks ingrained in the tile blurring together as I marched. I attempted to force my pounding heart to a more normal pace, but it was racing with a mind of its own.

"Well, I'll be damned," said the taller guy as we approached. "Dec, is that really you?"

From my periphery, I caught Declan's lip twitch before he twisted it into a smile. "Guilty as charged, Emmaus."

The guy slammed his big hand down on Declan's shoulder. "Good to see you. I didn't know you were back. Your father didn't say anything at today's meeting." He pointed at his companion. "You know Aristes, right?"

"Yeah, I think we met somewhere along the way."

"So are you back for good?" asked Emmaus. "Your father told us you were on some secret operation doing recon on the vampires."

"Oh yeah? That's what he told you, huh?"

Declan's fist clenched and unclenched at his side. I guess I wasn't the only one with no poker face. Or poker *hand* in this case.

I kept my head down as the guys continued to chitchat. Seriously? It's not like we weren't here on a super important and time sensitive mission. I suppressed the urge to elbow Declan in the gut.

"Man, Cassiel has been on us since you left." The tall blonde scowled and still managed to look breathtaking. "We're each expected to bring in two new human recruits a day. The generals just don't get it—there's no one out there anymore."

I bit back the urge to scream, tightening my hands into fists until my nails dug into my palms. Declan squirmed beside me.

Down the hall, a door swung open, and two human soldiers marched out. My eyes settled on familiar green eyes and sun-kissed skin. My heart stopped.

Asher.

My best friend's mouth dropped open as his gaze ran over me. His eyes flicked toward Declan, and it was as if I'd vanished. His serene green eyes lit up, an almost unnatural glow emanating from his irises. He and the guard next to him charged straight for us.

The two nephilim spun around at the slap of footfalls against the tile, both pairs of angelic blue eyes widening. Asher and the other human whizzed right by them and pummeled into Declan.

Before they collided, Declan released my arm and I darted out of the way. He hit the floor with the two soldiers on top of him. I was so shocked, I couldn't speak. My tongue was tied in knots as I stared slack-jawed.

One of the nephilim ran off yelling about an augmentation

gone wrong, and Declan's friend went for the other human guard. He yanked him off Declan and sent him flying against the wall.

Asher straddled Declan and pulled a pointed silver weapon out of his pocket. He thrust it down, and panic seized my chest. Declan twisted out of the way, and it just barely nicked his shoulder, a spurt of dark blood dripping down his arm. Declan's eyes smoldered a deep maroon. He wrapped his hands around Asher's neck and squeezed.

"Declan no! It's Asher." The words flew out of my mouth before I could stop them. I'd seen what he'd done to those vampires. Asher didn't stand a chance.

Declan glanced at me, his brows furrowed before his brain processed my words. He released his hold and let Asher drop to the ground.

I slid down beside him, cupping his face. "Asher, oh my God, Asher, it's really you."

A hint of a smile played on his lips, and then his expression darkened. "You shouldn't be here, Liv."

"I came for you," I choked out.

"It's too late for me." His bright green eyes dulled, and he removed my hands from his face, straightening his khaki jumpsuit.

"Asher?"

He stood and lunged for Declan again, brandishing the same silver weapon. Declan had been sitting on the floor wiping blood from his arm, but those killer nephilim instincts instantly flickered to life. Before Asher could bury the weapon in his chest, Declan's fiery angel sword burst to life in his palm. He swung the sword up and a blast of light sent Asher flying down the hallway.

"Declan stop!"

"I can't help it. He keeps coming at me. What am I supposed to do?" he growled.

Down the hall, the other human soldier was keeping Declan's

friend busy. The angel had him with his hands behind his back and shoved up against the wall.

Asher was about halfway down the corridor and back on his feet. He raced toward Declan.

What the hell is wrong with him?

I moved in front of Declan and squared my shoulders against the oncoming freight train that was my best friend. "Asher stop! He's my friend."

His lips twisted in disgust and fury burned his emerald eyes. "Do you even know what he is?" he hissed.

I chewed on my lower lip as shame burned my cheeks. "Yes." An angel. The *enemy*.

"I don't think you do." Asher shoved me to the side, and I lost my balance, smacking right into the wall.

My head spun as the scene went topsy-turvy. I lifted my hands to my head to stop the whirling and leaned against the white plaster.

Asher punched Declan in the face, and he staggered back with his hands raised. Asher murmured something, but I couldn't make it out. The whole scene was chaotic.

"Asher stop!" I yelled again, but deep down I knew it was futile. They'd done something to him. That wasn't my best friend. He'd been augmented like the rest of them. It was the only way he'd be able to go head-to-head with an angel.

He stalked toward Declan with the silver weapon in hand, and a cold gleam in his eye. He didn't even look at me. He charged at Declan again.

Declan blocked and ducked, avoiding his thrusts, but Asher had managed to back him into a corner.

I couldn't believe how strong my best friend was.

Footsteps echoed down the hall. I glanced down the corridor and Emmaus and the other soldier were gone. That meant more nephilim soldiers were on their way.

"Asher, please! We have to get out of here now." I tugged on his arm.

Nothing.

"We're here to rescue you—to bring you home."

My best friend continued his assault without sparing me a glance. The footsteps grew louder, and my heart beat in time with the relentless rhythm. We had to get out now. My throat constricted, but I swallowed down the debilitating emotion. "Declan, let's go. Just leave him." A pang of guilt sliced through my chest as I uttered the words.

Declan turned to look at me, and in that moment of distraction, Asher plunged the weapon down. Declan's hand shot out, and brilliant white light exploded from his palm. Asher's eyes widened as he soared through the air, his arms splayed out.

"No!" My scream echoed down the vacant corridor as Asher's head smashed against the far wall. The sickening snap of cracking bones reverberated down the hall.

My heart shattered.

"We have to go now!" shouted Declan as he scooped me up into his arms.

We raced past my best friend, who lay in a crumpled heap on the floor, his head twisted at an odd angle.

Bile crawled up my throat, leaving a streak of fire in its wake. Invisible fingers wrapped around my lungs tearing with razor sharp claws. *No. It can't be.* My gaze lingered on Asher as the scenery blurred until his image became more and more faint and finally disappeared.

"Asher..."

Out of the corner of my eye, a pair of white wings emerged, cocooning us in a glorious warm light. My breathing slowed, and my eyelids drooped as warmth enveloped me.

I closed my eyes, and my world faded to black.

CHAPTER 25

The sharp odor of liver and broccoli swirled in the air. I rubbed my nose, my eyelids fluttering open. A long tongue and furry snout hovered over me, warm dog breath in my face. "Duke!" I pulled his massive head into my chest and squeezed.

I sat up, my eyes straining to focus in the dark. Finally, my pupils adjusted and the details of Declan's living room coalesced to form a full picture.

How did I get back here?

I rubbed my head, a jumble of thoughts spinning in my brain. Then suddenly Asher's vacant green eyes flashed to the forefront. The entire terrible scene played out in my head in slow motion. *No.*

Tears blurred my vision, and an invisible weight crushed my chest. *Asher…*

My shoulders heaved as sorrow pierced a hot knife through my heart. A breath caught in my throat and I sobbed, burying my face in the couch pillow.

The creaking of the old wooden staircase drew my attention, and I released the cushion, quickly wiping the tears off my cheeks.

Declan appeared, his hair a mess with dark locks tumbling over his eyes. He slowly approached me, his maroon irises scrutinizing me from afar.

All the pain crushing my chest morphed into burning rage. Declan had done this. He killed Asher. The haze in my mind cleared, and every detail came into focus.

"You!" I leapt to my feet, anger igniting in my core. "How could you kill him?" I'd trusted Declan, and he'd done nothing but betray me from the beginning.

He stopped moving toward me and lifted his hands up. "I'm sorry, Liv. I didn't mean to. You know I didn't. He just kept coming at me, and I had to protect myself."

I shot him a narrowed glare, trying to infuse as much venom as humanly possible. "Protect yourself?" My voice raised a couple octaves. "You're a nephilim for God's sake! You're a million times stronger than he is. Aren't you practically immortal?"

He shook his head. "Liv, you saw him. He'd gone through augmentation. He wasn't just human anymore—not in strength anyway."

My mind rushed back to the white hallway and Asher's empty green eyes. And the way he spoke, it hadn't sounded anything like him. But at least he'd been alive, and now he wasn't. Because of Declan.

"I need to get out of here." I couldn't stand to be in the same room as the person responsible for killing my best friend. I barreled past him and up the stairs to get my stuff.

"Please, Liv. Where will you go?" Declan raced after me, his heavy feet stomping up the stairs behind me.

I reached the room I'd been staying in and tossed clothes in my backpack. He stood in the doorway, his eyes weary.

I threw the pack over my shoulder and stomped toward him. "Move."

He backed away with his hands raised, and I rushed down the stairs to the kitchen. I filled my bag with bottles of water and as many cans of food as I could carry, then grabbed Duke's leash. Declan watched from the entrance door. I ignored his piercing stare and collected everything I needed.

I was done trusting a half-angel.

"Come on, Duke." He dragged his lazy butt off the couch and followed me to the door.

Declan blocked the doorway, his arms stretched out.

"Get out of my way."

He shook his head, his lips turned down. "No."

"Declan, let me out of this house right now or I'll shoot you." I yanked the gun out of my backpack and pointed it at his chest.

His mouth dropped open. "Are you serious right now?"

"Dead serious." I released the safety, the click resounding in the silence.

"Liv, it's the middle of the night." He took a step back. "Have you even thought this through? Where are you going to go?"

"It's none of your business. I'm not your problem anymore. I never should've been." I lowered the weapon and tucked it into my waistband. Steeling my jaw, I fought back the tremor building inside me. "Now you can leave the city and keep hiding out from your father. Just keep pretending the world hasn't gone to hell and there's nothing you can do about it."

He huffed and raked his hands through his hair, pulling at the ends. "You don't understand; I already told you it's not that simple."

"I don't care, Declan. Just get out of my way so I can get as far away from you as I can." A knot lodged in my throat, and I swallowed hard to force it down.

"Fine. Do what you want." He stepped out of the way, and I shot by him with Duke at my heels.

The slam of the door behind me made my heart jump. I steadied my breathing and walked out into the quiet neighborhood. I still had a few hours till daybreak which meant I should get going now. It would be easier to avoid the angels in the dark.

I blinked back hot tears and checked the map to make sure I remembered the way and shoved it back into my backpack. Linc was the only person I could turn to now. I had no one else left.

~

DIM RAYS of light poked through the ever-clouded sky as I turned the corner, and the old church came into view. I patted Duke's head and his tongue shot out, covering my hand in slobber. The heaviness in my chest subsided just a bit.

I still couldn't think about the fact that I'd never see Asher again. He'd been my only reason for carrying on. I clenched my fists at my side and steeled my nerves. I had a new reason now—to end the angel's reign of terror.

I walked past the church and headed straight for the shack in the back parking lot. It was early, but I hoped Linc and his crew were awake. I moved toward the chipped yellowing doors, and my heart sank. The metal padlock was fastened shut.

I lifted my knuckle to the door and tapped. No answer. I waited a few seconds then knocked harder this time.

I didn't like being out in the open like this. I scanned the perimeter but as usual there wasn't a soul in sight. One more time. I banged on the door with both fists, praying to a God I wasn't even sure existed anymore that someone was still in there.

A terrible thought crossed my mind, squeezing my lungs in panic. What if Britt had gotten caught, and he'd been tortured to give up his friends' hideout? What if Declan had sold them all out somehow?

"Whoever's out there had better have a darn good reason for waking me up at the crack of dawn." A familiar southern drawl seeped through the shed doors, and I could finally breathe again.

"Linc, it's me, Liv. Please let me in."

A long thin file poked through the narrow gap between the doors. After a few attempts, it inserted itself into a nearly invisible hole in the back of the padlock. The mechanism clicked, and it popped open.

Linc opened the door a crack, and I had to restrain myself from jumping into his arms.

"You're okay?" he asked.

"I'm alive anyway."

He squinted his blue eyes as he searched behind me. "Britt's not with you?"

"No, we lost him. He didn't come back?"

He shook his head, his lips turning down. "Come on, get inside quick." He glanced at Duke, but didn't question me.

I followed him down the ladder into the underground passage. Jaxon and Jayse appeared from around a dim corner. Both wore matching sleepy expressions, dark bags under their eyes.

"Sorry I woke you guys up." I fiddled with the straps on my backpack and stared at the floor.

"Britt's not with you?" asked Jaxon.

"No. He was with Redson last I saw him. We got separated inside Arx."

His bright blue eyes widened. "You made it inside?"

I snagged my lower lip between my teeth. "Uh huh."

"What happened?"

"We couldn't find my friend in the barracks so Redson snuck us into Arx then we split up. Britt and Redson were supposed to check two floors and my friend, Declan, and I the other two. We ran into some nephilim soldiers and just barely made it out." I couldn't tell them about Declan, and I just didn't have it in me to admit what happened to Asher. If I spoke the words out loud, it would make them real. I wasn't ready for that.

"Damn," muttered Jayse. "I hope they made it out too."

Linc clapped his hand on his son's shoulder. "Britt's smart. He could be hiding out somewhere."

"I know he wanted to find his brother. Maybe he stayed back

to search some more?" It was a weak excuse, but at least it was something to hold on to.

"Where's your friend?" Linc's smoky blue eyes narrowed.

I crossed my hands over my chest, pulling my arms in to keep myself from falling apart. "We decided to go our separate ways." I paused, waiting for my voice to stop trembling. "He's looking for someone too."

Linc nodded. "I'm sorry you didn't find your friend, but if you're here for a second attempt, I can't help ya."

I shook my head and hardened my expression, then met Linc's inquisitive gaze head on. "I want to help with the mission. I'll do whatever it takes to take the angels down."

Linc's eyes bounced from Jaxon's to Jayse's and then back to me. "That's quite a big statement from a young girl."

Jayse cleared his throat and regarded his father. "Pa, she did make it in and out of Arx. That's no small feat."

"That is true." Linc scratched at his goatee, his eyes trained on me. "What can you bring to the team? We have limited resources and can't take just anyone. Most of our men are seasoned soldiers."

A trickle of sweat ran down my spine, my palms moist. I clenched my jaw, my decision made. "I can bring you a nephilim. He's the son of an angel stationed in Arx."

CHAPTER 26

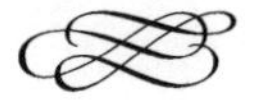

Acid churned in my stomach, and I wrapped my arms tighter around myself. I hadn't intended on blurting that out, but anger took control of my tongue and I couldn't stop it. Could I really sell Declan out?

Linc's silver eyebrows arched in surprise, his sons wearing matching shocked expressions. "You're kiddin' me."

I shook my head. "He trusts me. I can get him here if you guys can handle the rest."

Guilt burned through my chest as if someone had seared the word traitor across it. A small voice in the back of my head reminded me Declan had saved my life not once but three times. I ignored the annoying voice and shoved it down to the far recesses of my mind.

Asher was dead because of Declan, and that was all that mattered now.

Linc turned to his sons, a wry smile appearing on his face. "If we get a couple guys from the crew in on it and bring the nephilim to the warehouse, we might be strong enough to get some answers out of him."

Jaxon shook his head. "I don't know, Pa. We haven't tested out the vamp venom on many nephilim, what if it doesn't slow him down?"

My mind flashed back to the old silo and the vampire attack. Declan had passed out shortly after being bitten by that vampire. At the time, I thought it was from the blood loss.

"You guys have vampire venom?"

Jayse held his finger up to his lips. "It's our little secret. We discovered it was the only thing strong enough to do any damage to the angels."

"It's not reliable though," added Jaxon. "It has little effect on full-blooded angels and on the nephilim, it depends."

It probably depended on how much angel blood ran through their veins.

"It'll work on him," I muttered.

Duke barked, his big brown eyes judging me. It was like he knew I was selling out his friend.

"Okay then let's do this." Linc clapped me on the back and rubbed his hands together. "Give us a day to get the guys together. You can bring him to us tomorrow." He motioned to the ladder back up to ground level.

"Can I stay here till then?" I could only imagine what sort of underground system lay beyond this small room.

Linc grimaced, and his sons averted their eyes. "Sorry darlin', but rules are rules. I can't let you in until you're officially one of us." He put his hand on my shoulder and steered me toward the exit shaft. "Come back tomorrow at seven sharp, and we'll be ready for ya and the fiend."

Linc gave Duke a boost up and I followed behind, the weight in my chest back again.

"See you tomorrow," Linc's voice carried up from the tunnel as I emerged into the dim light of the toolshed.

Great. Now what?

A part of me wanted to stay in this shack for the rest of the day. Would they even notice if I did? I grunted and pushed the door open, not even bothering to refasten the padlock.

Jerks. At least they could've let me spend a few hours with them.

The murky daylight oozed all around me as Duke and I walked across the vacant parking lot. I had to get out of the street; I was too exposed.

"Come on, Duke. Let's go find a nice shady spot to hide out in."

He barked and licked my hand, and I headed toward the highway. The woods bordering it were the only ones I was familiar with.

Once we reached the cover of the towering oaks, my heartbeats returned to a more normal rate. I'd forgotten how unsettling the desolate streets and unending silence was when you were alone.

Don't think of Declan.

I couldn't help it though. As much as the cocky bastard irritated me at first, he'd gotten under my skin. Even after I'd discovered what he really was.

And now you're bartering with his life.

There it was—that annoying voice in my head. I felt like one of those cartoon characters with an angel on one shoulder and a devil on the other. Only in this messed up version, I wasn't sure who was worse: the angel or the devil.

Once the canopy of trees thickened, I slowed my pace. After a few minutes, I found a narrow rivulet and knelt down beside it to splash some water on my face. The crisp liquid awakened my dulled senses. It was easier not to think or feel when all there was left was pain. I pried my sneakers off and dipped my toes in the cool spring and groaned in pleasure.

I shrugged off my backpack and leaned up against a pine. "You hungry, boy?"

Duke sat beside me and lifted his paw, giving me five. "I'll take that as a yes." I rifled through the contents of my pack and pulled out a bottle of water and two cans of beans. "Sorry buddy, we're out of dog food."

He whined as I popped the tops off both cans and handed him one. I choked down the beans hoping they'd quell the uneasy sensation in my gut. After a few bites, I gave up.

The sudden flap of wings overhead sent ice through my veins. I pressed my back against the rough bark and quickly laced on my sneakers. Glancing up through the dark green canopy, luminous white wings circled just above the treetops. Radiant golden armor glinted in the sky, awakening a trail of goose bumps over my skin. Nephilim.

What were they doing out?

Declan had said there weren't any humans left to be hunted.

The flapping of wings grew stronger as the angel soldiers drew closer. *Crap*! I pulled Duke into my lap, praying he wouldn't bark. My heart pounded against my ribs as blood roared through my eardrums. I whipped my head back and forth, looking for somewhere to hide. Nothing but tall, unclimbable trees stretched in every direction.

Two nephilim soldiers alighted a few yards away, the snapping of fallen branches giving them away. I tucked my knees into my chest, trying to make myself invisible.

Duke's anxious eyes peered in the direction of the crackling foliage. I clasped my hand over his snout to keep him from barking and held my breath. The crunch of leaves grew closer, and a trickle of sweat ran down my back. The only thing between the nephilim and me was the thick tree trunk. I was as good as dead.

A whoosh of wind sailed over my head, and a third angel landed just to my right. I clapped my hand over my mouth as I recognized the dark unruly head of hair and piercing maroon eyes.

What was Declan doing here?

Without a glance in my direction, he addressed the pair of nephilim. "Nathanael wants you back at the tower immediately."

The tall blonde one with flowing locks like spun gold arched a brow. "We were sent out by General Cassiel. There have been reports of humans in the area."

"They were wrong."

The other angel took a step closer. "I don't think so. I saw something moving down here a few moments ago."

Declan glanced over at me and eyed Duke. "It must have been an animal." He ticked his head ever so slightly, his eyes boring into mine.

I shook my head. I knew what he was trying to tell me, but if I let Duke go there was no telling where he'd end up.

"Step out of the way, please," the dark haired nephilim got up into Declan's face. "Once we've searched the area, we'll return to headquarters."

Declan's hand shot out, shoving the guy squarely in the chest. "I've already told you it's not necessary."

"Aren't you Nathanael's son?" The blonde one stepped closer, cocking his head.

"No," he hissed.

Something tickled my arm. I looked down to find a spider crawling up my shoulder. I bit my tongue to keep the scream from exploding out of my mouth and flicked the hairy insect away. A twig snapped under my butt, and I froze.

Son of a v!

"There!" shouted the dark haired guy.

He pushed past Declan, and I leapt to my feet and ran. Duke took off beside me as I darted in between the trees, pumping my arms like mad. At any moment I expected strong arms to wrap around me and haul me into the air. But it never happened.

I slowed down to hazard a glance back. The murky forest was aglow with brilliant white and blue lights. Declan's sword danced between those of the nephilim, the clash of blades resounding through the stillness.

I couldn't see much at this distance, but from the looks of it, Declan was mopping up the floor with them.

I should've kept running. I knew that. The smart thing was to get the heck away from Declan and all the angels, but my feet were planted to the ground. He had saved me *again*.

The annoying voice in my head was back. *And you were going to betray him?*

"I'm still going to," I muttered aloud. Duke looked up at me and whined. "Don't look at me like that, boy. He killed Ash." My throat tightened, tiny invisible fingers wrapping around my neck.

The logical part of me knew Declan didn't mean to kill Ash, but my heart hurt too much to listen.

A high-pitched scream made my head spin back toward the fight. One of the angels was stretched out on the ground. Two luminous swords flashed through the trees as Declan, and the remaining nephilim went head to head. The guy was fast, but Declan was faster.

They moved behind a thick copse of trees, blocking my view. I hesitated for a moment before slowly walking back. I hated not being able to see what was going on.

I crept along the path, staying within the shadows, Duke at my heels. The clang of metal against metal reverberated in my skull, an occasional grunt breaking in between the clatter.

I neared the fallen angel and slowed. The magnificent creature was splayed out in the dirt, his long blonde locks muddied. Was he really dead? My eyes focused on the dark gaping hole on the left side of his chest. I cringed.

I moved closer, an odd fascination guiding my feet. There was no blood. Not a single drop anywhere around him.

Declan burst through the thicket, and my heart nearly burst out of my chest.

"Geez, Declan, you scared the crap out of me."

"Sorry."

I regarded him more closely. Bloody gashes covered his arms and a rather deep wound oozed dark red from his chest. "Are you okay?" I took a step toward him, then held back.

"Yeah, I'll be fine." He spat, and a stream of blood dripped down his chin.

"Is he dead?" I pointed at the angel.

"Yes." He frowned and crossed his arms against his chest.

Declan killed one of his own for me?

"How about the other guy?"

"You don't need to worry about him either."

Two of his own kind.

I wanted to ask him about the lack of blood, but the hollow look in Declan's eyes stopped me. It must have been an angel thing. "I guess I owe you another thank you."

"There's nothing to thank. Nothing good came out of this." His lips twisted into a scowl. He looked like he was going to be sick.

My hands longed to reach out to him and provide some sort of comfort, but I squeezed them at my sides. The mishmash of emotions swirling through my body was too much to get a handle on right now.

He killed Asher, but he'd saved my life countless times now. How could I reconcile those two actions?

I couldn't. Not yet anyway. "How did you find me?"

He shrugged and leaned up against a tree. "Not too many humans around so when I caught sight of those two, I figured it had something to do with you."

"Even after what I said to you? You were protecting me?"

He rubbed the back of his neck and stared at the ground. "You're a big enough problem as an ordinary human, you do *not* need to be augmented." A slight smirk pulled at his lips highlighting that damned irresistible dimple. "And besides, no matter how hard I try I can't seem to stay away from you."

A whole slew of butterflies battered my insides. What could I say to that? I swallowed down the traitorous flapping and refocused on what he'd said first. "Why didn't you tell me about the humans being augmented?"

He pushed out a slow breath. "I didn't want to disappoint you. I was hoping it hadn't happened to your friend."

"What was wrong with Asher? Why did he go after you like that?" I ignored the tremble in my voice as I spoke.

"I don't know."

Something dark flashed through his irises. I wasn't the only one with a bad poker face. There was still something he wasn't telling me. Why couldn't he be honest with me?

"I'm so sorry about Asher, Liv." He took a step closer and his hand reached up as if to touch me, but then he dropped it and tucked it into his pocket instead. "If there was anything I could do to take it back, I would. I never wanted to hurt you."

Tears pricked at my eyes, but I blinked them back. I couldn't cry again or I might never stop. "I know," I muttered. "I don't want to talk about him right now."

He nodded.

Could I forgive Declan for killing Asher? The sadness in his eyes made me want to, and yet a part of me felt that forgiving Declan would be betraying Asher. My heart was being torn in two.

After a few beats of silence, he caught my gaze. "So how'd it go with Linc?"

I narrowed my eyes. "How did you know that's where I went?"

"He's the only person you know in the area. Where else would you have gone?"

Somehow I had a feeling that wasn't how he'd figured it out. I think I had an angel stalker. "It went fine." I shoved my hands in my pockets and stared at the dirt. "I'm not sure that I want to stay with them." *Or sell you out to get in.*

"So what are you going to do?"

That was a good question. The only way Linc and his men

would allow me in would be if I gave them Declan. I peered up at the half-angel, a sadness emanating from those intense dark eyes. I couldn't do it. Even if he was an angel, and he had killed Asher, he didn't deserve to die.

I knew it was an accident, but that didn't make it hurt any less. But if I was being honest, losing Declan too would be more than I could handle. I had to forgive him... eventually.

"I don't know." The only thing holding me together had been my mission to find Asher, and now he was gone. I bit back the sob building in my throat.

"You could come with me to find my mom." His voice was so vulnerable, so unDeclan-like.

Before I could stop myself, the words popped out of my mouth. "Okay, sure."

CHAPTER 27

Clutching onto Declan's waist, my raven hair blowing in the wind, I seriously questioned my sanity. What was I doing? Going in search of Declan's missing mom?

I was following him around like some lost puppy dog was what I was doing. But what else was there? I didn't have anyone left. Nowhere else to go.

My arms tightened around Declan's waist without my consent.

Yup, I was definitely losing my mind.

The hour drive out of the city went by quickly with all the thoughts churning in my mind. I'd left D.C. without a word to Linc and his gang. A pang of guilt jabbed me in the gut. He'd been good to me, and I'd bailed on them. I never even found out if Britt made it out of Arx alive.

The rumble of the Harley slowed, pulling me from my inner musings. We veered off the highway onto a quiet street. A small green sign welcomed us to Elkins, West Virginia. He pulled the bike over to the shoulder and cut the engine. There wasn't another vehicle in sight; he could've just as easily stopped in the middle of the road.

"So now what?" I asked as Declan jumped off.

"I have to go check something out alone." He ticked his head toward the abandoned gas station. "You and Duke can wait here."

"What? No way." I slapped my hands on my hips. He wasn't just abandoning me in the middle of nowhere.

He placed his hands on my shoulders and pinned me with his hypnotic eyes. "I need to make sure it's safe. I don't want a repeat of what happened in the woods."

I huffed. Of course he had to bring that up. "Fine," I hissed through clenched teeth. "Come on, Duke."

Declan escorted us to the boarded-up gas station, yanking the plywood off the door. He went in first, the bells over the door jingling behind him as he scoped it out before allowing me to enter.

"It's clear. And it looks like there are snacks." For a second, the old Declan was back. I wasn't sure I liked this new broody one—even though I had a feeling his appearance was partially my fault.

I flicked my flashlight on and shone the light on the shelves of chips, pretzels, and other tasty treats. At least I'd have something to do while he was gone. "So where are you going exactly?"

"I have an address for my mom. I'm going to check it out before bringing you."

I nodded. "Okay." I wanted to believe him, but he'd lied to me so many times before I couldn't completely.

He regarded me, his expression hard. "I'm glad you came with me."

"Uh huh." It was all I could manage.

He headed toward the door then glanced back over his shoulder. "Don't go anywhere and be careful." Then he turned to Duke. "You, dog, watch her."

Duke barked and wagged his tail back and forth. *Traitor*!

"Just hurry up."

The door slammed, the bells clanging together, and I resisted the urge to run after him. *Get it together, Liv.*

I walked down the first row of snacks, eyeing my options. I

decided not to commit until I checked out the entire convenience store. After a few minutes, I had an armful of sweet and salty snacks. I settled down in a corner and popped open the first bag, Duke sitting beside me. His big tongue lolled out, slobber dripping from his mouth.

"Okay, okay, just one." I threw a chip toward his muzzle and he caught it midair, his jaw snapping shut. He crunched happily and settled down next to me.

Sometimes I was jealous of Duke. His life was so simple.

THE RUMBLE of the Harley pulling up the drive sent me racing to the glass door. Declan tugged off his helmet and leapt from the motorcycle, his expression as dark as his black t-shirt. As he stalked up the walkway, I wondered why he even bothered to wear a helmet. Weren't nephilim practically immortal anyway?

He jerked the door open and scowled. I decided now was not the right time to question his helmet wearing.

"You didn't find her?"

"No," he growled.

"Maybe she went out for a walk?"

He ground his teeth together. "Doubtful." He stomped around the store and grabbed a few chocolate bars before turning back to me. "Come on. I want to go back to her place and look around some more. Maybe I can find a clue as to where she might have gone."

"Okay."

The three of us got back on the motorcycle, and Declan tore out of the gas station lot. It wasn't often he was in a dark mood like this, but I didn't like it one bit. It reminded me of the fierce angel lingering just below the surface. The one that killed Asher. When he was his fun, bubbly self, it was easy to forget what he really was.

We reached Declan's mom's house in no time. He cut the engine, and I stared up at the cute one story home. It was the same powder blue as the row house in D.C. only in much better condition. Apparently the fighting hadn't encroached on this quiet suburban town.

Declan pushed the picket fence open and parked the motorcycle in the circular driveway. "Come on, get inside." He rushed me up the porch steps and into the foyer of the quaint home. Once we were inside, he released a sharp breath. "I don't think we should stay long, just in case my father's got eyes on the place." He tilted his head up to the ceiling. "I did a quick sweep before bringing you here and it was clear, but that doesn't mean it'll stay that way."

"You mean you flew?" I pointed out the window toward the gray sky.

"Yes. That's what these are for." A brilliant light exploded from his back, and a pair of snow-white wings unfolded.

My breath hitched, and I could've sworn Duke's eyes bulged out too. I didn't think I'd ever get used to him doing that.

Light crimson stained Declan's cheeks, and the magnificent wings folded behind his back. "I'm going back up there for another look. Can you check in here and see if you find anything?"

"You're going to leave me alone again?" I cringed at the whininess in my tone. What was up with that? I could totally handle myself. "It's just that you said angels could be back..."

He frowned and ran his hand through the dark mop of wavy hair. "No, you're right. If my father has discovered she's missing, he'd surely have soldiers out searching for her. We don't want to risk them finding you instead."

"What's the deal with your parents?" The words burst out of my mouth as I lowered myself onto the couch. "I mean, does your dad really care about her? He took the time to hide her when the world went to hell, but then why would she have run off?"

"I don't know." He snagged his lower lip between his teeth. "All I know is that I thought she was dead, and now I know she's not. Whatever the circumstances were for her leaving my dad and me, I have to find out." He paced the length of the small living room, his tall frame nearly brushing the ceiling fan. After a few more circles, he turned to me. "Okay, quick look around the house and then we'll go."

I nodded and rose.

"There are two bedrooms and a bathroom that way." He pointed down a hallway. "You check those and I'll take the living room and kitchen."

I started toward the corridor then turned back. "What am I looking for exactly?"

"Anything that might lead us to where my mom could have gone."

Sure, easy peasy. It's not like I was going to find a bus ticket receipt or something. At least this was a distraction from thinking about Asher.

My sneakers sunk into the soft carpeting as I walked noiselessly to the first door on the right. A flowery comforter covered a queen-sized bed with pale pink walls. A picture frame on the nightstand caught my eye. It was the same photo as the one from Declan's room in his childhood home. I stared at the smiling brunette, and my chest tightened. If my mom were still alive, I'd do anything to find her too. Where are you Mrs.—it occurred to me I didn't even know Declan's last name. Did angels even have last names?

I rifled through a few loose sheets of paper on the nightstand —bills from over a year ago when we had electricity and cable. I searched the rest of the room but came up with nothing besides a couple of super cute pictures of Declan as a baby. I tucked those into my jeans' pocket to tease him about later.

I was about to walk out of the room when a closed door behind the entry caught my eye. The closet. I pulled it open and shuffled through some dresses and jackets. Something against the back wall got my attention. I pushed aside the clothes, and my jaw dropped.

Newspaper clippings, sketches, and Internet articles were taped across the back wall of the closet. Had Declan seen this? I shoved my way deeper into the closet and scanned the images. They were of the angel-vampire war. Most of them were from the beginning, but some must have been underground sources with dates as recent as a few weeks ago. It reminded me of one of those crime boards you saw on police detective TV shows.

"Declan, I think you need to come in here."

He was at my side in seconds. "What did—" His eyes went wide as his gaze followed mine. He ran his finger over the images, his jaw practically unhinged.

Below all the articles were handwritten notes. Some had names and others just a series of lines and arrows. None of it made any sense.

"Who's Nathanael?" It was the name repeated most on the wall schematic. "Angel of fire?"

Declan cleared his throat and shifted his weight from foot to foot. "Nathanael is my father."

My eyes ran over all the black and white typography until it blurred. "Your dad is one of the head angels?" All the air rushed out of my lungs, making my head spin. According to these articles, he was one of the angels who led the war on the vampires—and caused the near annihilation of the human race.

He nodded, refusing to meet my eyes.

"How could you not tell me that?" I forced my voice to stay calm when I really wanted to curse at him. Sometimes I wondered if anything true ever crossed his lips.

"What's the point? So that you'd hate me more?"

"You can't avoid telling me things that you think I'm not going to like. It's still lying!" I crossed my arms over my chest, trying to hold the anger in.

"I'm sorry, okay? I told you I'm not proud of who I am. That includes my father."

Just great. Not only had I managed to make friends with a nephilim, but I had to pick the son of one of the men responsible for all of this destruction.

Declan glanced back at the wall and rubbed at his scruffy chin. "It looks like she's been tracking him from the start."

Okay… I guess our lying conversation was over.

"Do you know what this means?" I pointed at the mess of lines and symbols on post-it notes.

"No."

Next to it was a page torn out of a book. I squinted to get a closer look at the tiny writing. No wonder I couldn't make it out; it wasn't in English.

"Do you know what language this is?"

Declan scrutinized the page. "It looks like ancient Aramaic, but that language has been dead for centuries."

"Well whatever it is, it seems pretty important to your mom." It was highlighted in neon yellow and circled about a hundred times. "Did you find anything in the rest of the house?"

"No. You definitely hit the jackpot over here. I checked the other bedroom too, and it was empty."

"So now what?"

"Now we fly."

CHAPTER 28

Glorious wings extended out behind Declan's back emitting a soft glow. His head tilted up peering into the darkening sky, and I dipped my head back to follow his line of sight.

"What are you looking at?" There wasn't a thing up there besides thick gray clouds.

"Just making sure the skies are clear." He turned around to get a hundred and eighty degree view, giving me a close-up of his wings. A hint of silver threaded through the feathers along the edges, and my fingers ached to touch them. Before Declan, I hated wings. Their incessant droning signified war and destruction, but on him it was different.

Before I could stop myself, I gently ran my hand over the velvety feathers. It was like sinking into a fluffy cloud. Declan shuddered, a slight groan escaping his lips.

"Sorry," I muttered, snatching my hand back.

He turned around and regarded me with smoldering irises. "No, don't be. It felt good. *Really* good." He gave me an indulgent smile, and his dark brow rose into a mischievous arc. "You ready?"

Sure, just give me a second for my lungs to start working again. I still couldn't believe I'd agreed to this. About a million butterflies fluttered to life in my stomach. "Okay, ready."

He took my hand and spun me around so my back was against his chest. "Now put one foot on each of mine."

I held onto his arm for balance and did as instructed. His other arm slid around my waist pressing me into his body. My stomach wasn't the only organ fluttering now. I didn't know what to do with my arms so they hung awkwardly at my side.

"Here we go!" Declan bent his knees and pushed off the ground.

The earth fell away, and my stomach dropped. My breath hitched as the cool night air whooshed over my skin. My hands shot out to grab a hold of something and ended up clasping onto Declan's arms encircling my waist. His magnificent wings flapped noiselessly, glowing in the periphery.

I hazarded a look down, and my pulse spiked. The cute blue house got smaller and smaller until it looked like nothing more than a tiny dot amidst the greenery. My head spun, and I squeezed my eyes shut.

"You okay?" Declan asked, tightening his hold around my torso.

"Yeah," I rasped out.

"Don't forget to breathe. It'll help."

A smile cracked my lips and for a second I tried to enjoy the feeling of weightlessness as we soared higher into the sky. The further up we went the easier it was to forget everything below.

Declan tilted his body forward so we were almost parallel to the ground. My toes curled in my sneakers struggling to hold on. The ground zipped by beneath us as Declan flew just under the clouds. His gaze was set to the tiny houses and streets below. I squinted to focus, but at this height it was useless. I couldn't make out a thing.

My foot slipped off of Declan's, and I had to bite back the scream that threatened to peal out.

"If you're not comfortable, you could say so," he whispered into my ear, his warm breath sending a chill up my spine.

"Huh? No I'm—"

"You're practically cutting off my circulation with your nails."

I glanced down at the red half-moon marks covering his arms. My fingers were so tightly clenched around his forearms, my knuckles were white. "Oops. Sorry."

I relaxed my grip and struggled to slow my racing heart.

"Here, maybe this will be better."

Before I could object, Declan scooped up my legs and shifted his arm behind my back, cradling me into his chest. My arm snaked around his neck, my fingers digging into his shoulder.

"Better?"

As silly as I felt being carried like a baby, I had to admit it was better. "Yeah, thanks." With Declan's strong arms wrapped around me, hundreds of feet in the air, I felt the safest I had in awhile. "So do you see anything down there?"

"No. I was hoping I'd catch some nephilim soldiers scouting the area, but there's no one."

"Well keep looking. Now that I've gotten the hang of it, flying's pretty amazing."

"I'm glad *you've* gotten the hang of it." He shot me a smirk before returning his attention to the ground.

My fingers curled into his shirt, but I wasn't scared anymore. My breathing returned to normal, and I took in the rolling terrain below us. I'd never been on an airplane before and if we weren't in the middle of an apocalypse I could see enjoying this sort of thing. Everything was so quiet and peaceful up here.

I lost track of time, my head buried in Declan's chest, breathing in the calming lavender scent of his t-shirt. My stomach flip-flopped alerting me of our descent, and I snapped out of the peaceful haze. Inky darkness covered the land; only Declan's wings provided us with a warm glow.

"We're going back?"

"Yeah. There's no one out here. If anyone had been looking for Mom, they're long gone now." The tendons in his jaw tightened, and his lips pressed into a thin line.

"You'll find her, Declan. I know you will."

His enormous wings flapped faster as we dipped toward the ground. I wrapped both arms around his neck as the wind whipped dark strands of hair across my face.

It was full night when we reached the small blue house. Declan lowered me onto the porch, and my knees wobbled for a second. He grabbed my hands to steady me, eyeing me with those mesmerizing maroon irises. His snow-white wings encircled him in a heavenly glow. He was beautiful.

"You okay?"

"Yeah, I'm fine. It must be the sudden change of altitude." My head spun, and I clutched onto Declan's forearms. "Whoa. Sorry about that." I glanced up, and his mouth was inches from mine.

I licked my lips, my throat suddenly dry.

The air crackled, invisible sparks filling the space. My fingers tingled from the heat emanating from his skin.

He dipped his head and slowly closed the distance between us.

My lips parted, glancing up at hooded eyes under a curtain of dark lashes as I inched closer.

The front door creaked open, and we jumped, Declan pulling me behind him. A familiar brunette peeked through the crack in the door, her eyes wide.

"Mom?"

The woman pushed the door open the rest of the way and squinted, her gaze running up and down the big nephilim standing in front of me. "Declan, is it really you?"

Declan's chest heaved, and he sucked in a breath. "It's me, Mom." He released me and pulled her into an embrace, nearly knocking the door off its hinges in the process.

"Come in, come in children." She eyed the dark sky then ushered us inside.

Duke trotted out to greet us as soon as we entered. I gave him a quick pat, relieved he was okay.

Declan's mom looked to me then back at Duke. "I was wondering where he'd come from."

"Mom, where have you been?" Declan sat her down on the couch. His eyes never left her as if he were scared she'd disappear if they did.

"I've been right here." She pointed at the floor.

"Mom, it's been ten years. What happened? Why did you leave?"

I suddenly felt like I should be anywhere but here. This wasn't a conversation that should be had in front of a stranger. I slowly backed up out of the living room, planning on hiding out in the extra bedroom.

"Liv, stop."

Declan's voice halted my feet, halfway out of the room.

"I want you to be here for this. Maybe it'll help clear things up."

Um. Okay. I nodded and sat down on the chair across from Declan and his mom.

Declan squeezed her hand, his eyes intent on her face. "Please, Mom, tell me what happened."

The lines around her dark eyes deepened, and her lower lip trembled. "It wasn't my choice." A tear rolled down her cheek, and Declan swept it away with his thumb. She drew in a breath and began once again. "I don't even know where to begin." She pressed Declan's hand to her cheek. "I overheard your father talking to Cassiel one night; they were planning this war all those years ago. The vampires had to be stopped, but the price the humans would pay was clear from the start. I begged Nathanael to reconsider, but he said there was nothing he could do. The plans had been put in motion, and it was only a matter of time. The more I learned about their mission, the more sure I became of how wrong it was." She paused, wringing her hands together.

Ten years ago—the angels had been plotting this war for that long? But how was that possible if the vampires attacked first?

She looked up at her son. "Your powers hadn't even surfaced yet. To me, you were just a little boy—a human like me. When your father wouldn't listen to me, I ran with you. We didn't make it far."

Something flashed across Declan's dark gaze. "The road trip? To Disney World, when I was nine?"

She nodded and ran her hands over her damp cheeks.

"I remember we got into a car accident on the way and had to turn back." He furrowed his brow, sitting forward on the couch. "I never got to see Mickey."

His mom pursed her lips. "It wasn't an accident. Nathanael sent nephilim after us. They ran us off the road and nearly killed you. When we got home, your father banished me. If I ever tried to see you, he said he'd—" She choked back a sob.

"He threatened to kill you?" Declan hissed.

She shook her head. "No. He said he'd kill *you*."

He lurched back as if he'd been punched in the stomach. My own breath hitched. How could a father threaten to kill his own son?

"That son of a—" Declan bit back the curse with a growl. "All this time he made me believe you had died."

"How did you find out she was still alive?" I couldn't help myself; the words just tumbled out.

Declan turned to me, his face blank as if he'd forgotten I was there. "My father told me." He stood, curling his fists at his side. "When I informed him I didn't want any part of this anymore, he tried to stop me. He said there was something I needed to know. I blew him off and left anyway. Then he had some nephilim track me down a few weeks later. They gave me a note from my father with my mom's address. It was meant to be a peace offering."

"And that's when you met me?"

He nodded. "A short while after."

Declan had wasted all that time helping me when he knew his mother was alive. My chest tightened as a flurry of emotions swelled. Why would he do that for me?

Declan's mother stood and gave me a smile. "My how rude of me, I never introduced myself." She held out her hand. "I'm Sammarah McGrath." Her thin dark brows knitted together as she scrutinized me, an odd expression on her face. Then she forced a smile, returning to normal.

"Liv Graciene. Nice to meet you too." I reached for her hand, but her fingertips slipped right through mine. Declan moved faster than I'd ever seen, catching her before she hit the floor.

"Mom?" He held her in his arms, her face pale against his chest.

I ran to the kitchen to get a glass of water. I wasn't sure why; it seemed like the helpful thing to do.

Declan carried her down the hallway to her bedroom, and I followed a few steps behind.

"It's only a dizzy spell," she murmured, her eyelids fluttering. "I need a little rest is all."

Declan lowered her onto the bed, the old mattress sinking in under her measly weight. He pulled the covers over his mom and tucked her in, kneeling on the floor next to her. I stared at the glass in my hand, again feeling like I was intruding on a private moment.

"Do you need anything?" he asked. "Water?"

"No, I'm fine, son." Her eyes moved to me. "You can leave that on the nightstand in case I get thirsty."

I set it down and walked out of the room to give them some privacy. Walking out into the living room, a million thoughts swirled in my head. The one I couldn't shake no matter how hard I tried was what kind of a man would kill his own son? What chance did we have against the angels if they had so little regard for human life?

The more I heard about Nathanael, the more obvious it became that he held a high position in the angel hierarchy.

Declan had never admitted it, but what if his father was in charge of Arx?

Declan's elevated voice drifted down the hall. I jumped up and crept back toward Sammarah's room.

I wasn't eavesdropping; I was just concerned.

"Forget about it, Mom. We can talk about it later. I shouldn't have even brought it up."

"You can't ask me something like that and not expect me to worry." Sammarah's voice sounded like it was on the verge of hysterics. "Did something happen to you?"

"No. It was a hypothetical question. I thought you might know... Never mind. Get some rest."

The mattress squeaked as he rose, and I darted back into the living room. Grabbing a book off the coffee table, I buried my nose in it and sank down into the sofa.

What had Declan been talking about?

He skulked into the sitting room, his forehead creased with worry. He pushed his dark curls back and slumped down on the couch next to me.

"Is she okay?"

He frowned, his lips turning into a cute pout. "She won't let me use my angel light on her."

"I'm sure she'll be fine. She's probably just emotionally drained." I squeezed his hand and gave him what I hoped was a reassuring smile.

"Yeah, I guess." He glanced down at our entwined fingers and his eyes darkened. "Are you okay with everything?"

I shrugged. Was I over the fact that my best friend was dead? No. Was Sammarah a good distraction? Yes.

"Just because my family drama has taken center stage, doesn't mean I'm not here for you if you ever want to talk about Asher or your parents." The sincerity in his eyes tugged at my heart.

"Thank you." My fingers tightened around his. Talking about

them would be like opening floodgates I wasn't ready to unleash. I was petrified I'd drown in the deluge.

We sat in a comfortable silence until my lids began to droop. I stifled a yawn and sat up straighter.

"You don't have to stay up with me if you're tired. I'll take the couch and you can sleep in the extra bedroom."

"No, I'm fine." I rubbed my eyes and turned to face him.

He reached his hand out and tucked a dark strand of hair behind my ear. His hand lingered for a moment then slid down to my shoulder. My pulse quickened at the warmth of his fingers on my skin.

"You're not fine. You're exhausted, Liv. Go to sleep."

"As long as you're okay?"

"I'm good. Plus I got Duke here to keep me company."

Duke lifted his head and peered up over the couch. Declan scratched behind his big ears, and he whimpered contentedly.

"Okay, I'll see you in the morning." I stood and made my way down the corridor. Glancing back, Declan's intense gaze met mine. A wave of heat coursed through my body as our eyes locked. All the moisture in my mouth vanished, and I swallowed hard.

I dropped my gaze to the floor, unable to hold contact with those smoldering maroon irises a second longer.

"Night, Liv," he called out, and I scurried around the corner into thc guest bedroom.

I shut the door and leaned on it for a moment to catch my breath. What was that look? *Get it together, Liv*. I shook my head, clearing my mind of the fuzzy feelings lurking below the surface. I needed sleep; I was obviously starting to hallucinate. I slipped out of my sneakers and jeans and crawled into the bed.

I do not have feelings for Declan. I do not *have feelings for a half-angel.*

I repeated the mantra until my eyelids grew so heavy I was forced to give up the fight.

CHAPTER 29

"They're coming! They're coming!"

Frantic shrieks echoing across the house snapped me wide awake. I jumped out of bed and raced toward the screams.

In the living room, Declan's mom, Sammarah, had a hold of his collar and was shouting into his face.

"Mom, calm down. Who's coming?" Declan's eyes were wide, his hair tousled. He'd obviously just woken up too.

"Them. They're after me. They're always watching…" She buried her face into her son's chest and sobs wracked her thin frame.

I took a step closer and she spun toward me, wild dark eyes blazing. "It's not safe. We have to hide—all of us." She grabbed Declan's hand and then mine and led us down the corridor.

"Mom, where are you going?"

"They won't find us. Not here." She barreled into her bedroom, pulling us along with her and whipped open the closet door. Pushing aside the clothes, she squirmed her way to the far corner. She bent down and shoved two large suitcases out of the way revealing a hidden hatch on the floor.

As she yanked it open, Declan and I stared at each other in shock. Was this where she'd been hiding yesterday when we arrived?

"Come now. There's no time." She jumped down the shaft before Declan could stop her.

If someone were coming, Declan would've known. Wouldn't he? His super angel hearing would've alerted us, but there was nothing in his expression that confirmed his mom's panic.

He grabbed my hand and pulled me to the edge of the opening. A ladder disappeared down into the darkness.

"I'll go first. Follow me."

I nodded as he started the descent. Slowly, I climbed down, rung by rung, the ominous squeaking sending a chill skittering up my spine. I wished I'd had my flashlight.

As if Declan had heard my thoughts, he extended his hand and angel light came to life in his palm. He jumped down, and the glow illuminated the dark space. I rushed down the last few rungs and hit the ground with a thud.

What was this place?

Declan moved in a circle, shining his angel light around the secret chamber. Thick black mud made up the walls and floor, the earthy scent filling my nostrils. An old wooden table and chair sat along one of the walls and a metal cot ran along the opposite side. Sammarah's huddled form took shape in the far corner.

Declan ran to her, sliding down to sit beside her. "Mom, what is this place?"

"It's my little secret. No one can find me here." A smile spread her pale lips. "They think I'm gone, but I'm not. I've always been right here."

The look on Declan's face nearly broke my heart as he peered up at me. His mom had completely lost it. Where was the sane woman we'd met last night?

I circled the room, Declan's angel light providing a dim glow that illuminated the dank space. As I neared the wooden table, a stack of papers caught my eye. I flipped through them as Declan attempted to calm down his mom. He was whispering to her now, his palms glowing with healing angel light.

The pages revealed more scribbles, similar to the ones I'd discovered in the closet yesterday. We should've known there was something wrong with her when we'd found those. But she'd seemed so normal.

Soft footfalls drew my attention. Declan's mother was draped across his arms, a peaceful smile gracing her delicate features as he carried her to the cot. From up close, the resemblance between her and her son was more obvious. Not only did they share the same raven hair and dark eyes, but Declan's nose and cheeks were simply a more pronounced version of his mother's.

"She's asleep," he whispered over her still form, his voice gravelly as he moved beside me. I'd never seen this side of Declan before. A part of me liked this new vulnerable side, but the other just wanted to see the happy, joking one back.

"Should we take her back upstairs?"

He shook his head. "The shaft is too narrow for my wings. It'd be hard to get her back up the ladder without waking her." He turned and walked to the corner, lowering her onto the cot and covering her with a blanket.

He appeared over my shoulder as I rifled through the notes. "What did you find?"

"More of the same. Not much of it makes any sense to me."

He picked up a few pages and scanned them. "It looks like more Aramaic."

"Shouldn't you be able to read that, you know, as an angel?"

"First of all, I'm a nephilim. Second of all, I was born in the 21st century not in the first." He smirked and for a second I got a glimpse of the old Declan. "If I went back to the tower, I could find someone to translate it. I still have some friends there."

I shivered at the thought. "Maybe we can just ask your mom about it?"

The tendons in his jaw twitched. "Didn't you see her, Liv? I don't know what they've done to her, but she's not in her right mind. All of this could be a bunch of insane scribbles for all we know."

"But the Aramaic? Don't tell me your mom would've written those?"

He blew out a frustrated breath. "No, you're right. She wouldn't have."

I stared at the scrawled writing, willing it to turn into something legible, but no such luck. "So now what?"

"I don't know. I'm hoping my angel light will help, but I've never tested it out for mental illness."

"Are you sure that's what it is?" I drummed my fingers on the wood table.

"No. I'm not sure about anything, but what are you thinking?"

I gulped. "The augmentation ray and the weird way Asher was behaving before—" I cut myself off before I started getting choked up. "What if the angels did something to her?"

He shook his head. "No way. There's no way my father would've let them hurt her."

I opened my mouth, but then snapped it shut. His father had threatened to kill him. Why would his mother be any safer?

"You're wrong, Liv." He stepped closer, his wide shoulders bearing over me. "Maybe he never loved me, but I know he loves her."

"Okay." I raised my hands up. "They're your parents so I guess you'd know." Or was he just too blind to see what a monster his father was? I yawned and glanced at my watch. Not even five in the morning yet. "I'm going back to sleep."

"Right." He sat on the chair and flipped through the papers as I walked toward the ladder. "Hey, Liv…"

"Yeah?"

"Maybe you should stay down here, just in case."

"You think your mom was right about the angels coming?"

He shrugged. "I don't know, but I'd rather not risk it." He stood and grabbed a few blankets from the pile by the cot. Arranging them along the wall by the table, he patted the ground when he was finished. "Sorry for dragging you into this."

I sat beside him, my back against the cool dirt wall. "If you're apologizing for this, then I guess I have a lot to apologize to you for." I was the one that made him come to Arx with me in the first place. He'd killed vampires and angels for me. Even Asher's death was partially my fault. I slid my hand in his. "I suppose we can call it even."

A small smile curled his lip, and his fingers tightened around mine. "Get some rest. I'll keep watch just in case."

My lids were already sagging. I leaned my head against Declan's shoulder and drifted off to sleep.

THE CRACKLE of crinkling pages drew me from a fitful sleep. My neck ached as I sat up and took in my surroundings. *Oh right, secret underground room.* Declan sat in the chair beside me, poring over the sheets scattered across the table.

"Did you get any sleep?" I asked.

He turned, dark shadows under his red-rimmed eyes. I guessed not.

"No. But I think I'm starting to get this."

I glanced over at the cot where his mother still slept peacefully. I stood and joined him beside the table. There were five stacks of papers now and some passages were underlined in red. "So what did you figure out?"

"I found this upstairs." He pulled a thick leather-bound book from under the table. Frilly golden script lined the cover.

"What is it—Aramaic for dummies?"

He cracked a smile. "Kind of. I used it along with my very basic knowledge of Aramaic as well as my more vast understanding of Latin to decipher some of the passages she'd highlighted."

"And?" I bounced on my tiptoes.

"It seems all of this had been prophesied hundreds of years ago." He pointed at a rather long passage. "The rise of the vampires was foretold here, along with the resulting war that would ensue. They knew it would nearly wipe out mankind."

"Seriously?" I bent down to get a better look. Not like it helped because I still didn't understand a thing.

"It was supposed to be a cleansing of all the evil on earth. The humans that survived were the ones deemed worthy enough to repopulate the world."

"What?" This was some crazy cult-like babble. How could they exterminate the whole human race like we were just collateral damage?

"At least there's talk about survival and moving forward."

"Does it say how we're supposed to do that with the angels and vampires still roaming around?"

"I haven't gotten quite that far yet."

"Declan?" A quiet voice called out from across the room.

He shot up from the chair and raced over to the cot. "Mom, how are you feeling?"

"I'm just fine, son." The crazed look in her eyes from earlier was gone. She scanned the room and frowned. "What are we doing down here?"

"You don't remember?" He sat beside her and held her hand.

She shook her head, a vacant look in her eyes.

"You woke up in the middle of the night and brought us down here. You said 'they' were coming. Who were you talking about?"

Her lip quivered, and she glanced up at me as if searching for an answer. "I don't know." She sucked in a breath. "Sometimes I lose time. I forget..."

"Do you know what all this is?" I motioned to the stacks of

paper. I knew I shouldn't intrude on this family moment, but I couldn't help myself.

"My work," she muttered.

"Is that why you left dad? You'd figured out what was going to happen."

"Yes." She clasped her other hand on top of Declan's. "I found most of it in Nathanael's library; the rest I pieced together myself over the years. I tried to warn people, but no one would listen. I spent a few years in an institution because of it."

I suppressed a gasp. This poor woman had been through so much. Could any of this be true? Considering the source, it seemed unlikely.

She sat up and cupped Declan's cheeks, and my heart clenched as memories of my own mom flooded my thoughts. I wrapped my arms tight around my torso, holding myself together.

"Declan, there's still hope," she whispered. "There's a way to end all of this."

"What? How?" My heart slammed against my ribcage, a sliver of optimism unfurling in my chest.

She straightened her back, her dark chocolate eyes intense. "Everything that has happened was foretold. It was part of a bigger plan that I have yet to make sense of, but there is a solution."

"What kind of a solution?" asked Declan. He sat at the edge of the cot, his knuckles white from gripping his knees.

She stood, shaky at first, and marched to the table. Flipping through the pages, she pulled one out of the stack and held it up. Declan and I both rushed to her side. She ran her finger over a section that was underlined and dotted with question marks. "This."

I inched closer to the yellowing page, but couldn't make a single word out of the strange letters. Declan moved next to me and peered at the foreign words.

"I didn't see this before. It references the *sakra lampiada*?"

"The what?" It looked like a bunch of scribbles to me.

"That would be the approximate phonetic pronunciation from Aramaic of the shield of light."

Sammarah's eyes lit up. "That is the answer to the survival of the human race."

What? Was I the only one that was completely lost here?

A deep line formed between Declan's brows as he stared at the text. "You believe this is real?" He eyed his mom skeptically.

"Everything else I discovered has come to pass. Why wouldn't this?"

I threw my hands out. I was tired of being left out of this conversation. "Stop. Can someone please explain what the heck is going on?"

Declan turned to me, his dark brows furrowed. "It mentions a shield with the power to stop both vampires and angels; one that only a human can wield, but it's pretty vague."

"Only a special human," Sammarah cut in. "One with the gift of *kharashuot*."

Declan glanced at his mother, his eyebrow arched. "Magic?"

Okay it was official, Declan's mom was nuts. Humans didn't have magic; everyone knew that.

"*Kharashuot* meant many things in Aramaic. It's important not to be so literal when translating a centuries-old language. From what I've gathered, it could simply mean gifted or charmed."

"Well that doesn't really make it any clearer," I muttered.

"And how would we find that one person?" Declan was pacing now.

A sparkle ignited in her eyes, brightening her whole expression. "My dear boy, it's not only one person. It's one family bloodline, chosen by the creator millennia ago to save the future of mankind. In his infinite wisdom, he bestowed this power onto a human who would carry that gift through their bloodline for generations. They would ultimately overcome the immortals who'd gone astray."

My head spun. This was some major crazy.

"Mom, maybe you should sit down." Declan pulled out the wooden chair, motioning to it.

She shook her head, the smile across her face twisting into a frown. "You don't believe me either?"

"I want to. It just seems so far-fetched."

That was an understatement.

"Even if we did believe you Mom, how would we ever find this special family line? How do we know they haven't all been killed by now?"

"Because God would never be that cruel." She stared up at her son with such sincerity that I wanted to believe her.

Heck, she probably did believe what she was saying was true. Wasn't that what happened when you went crazy?

She laid her hand on his chest and smiled. "I've been chosen, Declan. It's in *my* blood."

Declan's eyes went cartoon character wide, and I'm sure my expression matched his.

"Mom, no—" Declan's head spun toward the ladder leading up the shaft and he clenched his jaw, cursing. "Angels," he hissed.

My stomach dropped as icy terror rushed through my veins. Sammarah had been right. They *were* coming.

"Both of you stay down here and do not come up for any reason. No talking either; you know how sensitive angel hearing is." Declan took his mom's hand and placed it in my trembling one. His steely gaze locked onto mine and heat swirled in my middle. "Take care of each other."

I nodded, afraid of what might come out if I opened my mouth.

He shot up the ladder, the glow of his sword lighting up the dark tunnel for a moment before vanishing. The hatch slammed shut and silence surrounded us.

CHAPTER 30

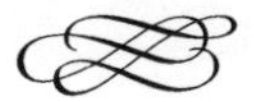

Sammarah and I sat shoulder to shoulder against the rough dirt wall. Declan had only left five minutes ago and yet it seemed like a lifetime. I strained my ears to make out a sound, but the thick layers of dirt and concrete between us and the outside were impenetrable. Sammarah had created a highly effective hideout.

Anxiety churned my stomach, acid bubbling up in my gut. What if something happened to Declan? What if they'd killed him already?

Sammarah's long thin fingers wrapped around my hand and squeezed. It was warm, comforting and familiar. My chest tightened as the pang of my mother's loss crept to the surface.

"Everything will be all right," she whispered in my ear.

I wanted to believe her, but the little voice in my head reminded me she was crazy. She thought she was the one that could end all of this. That she came from some special mythical bloodline that could wield a legendary shield and save us all.

And yet, with her fingers tight around mine, I couldn't deny the calming sensations rolling through my body. It was almost like Declan's angel healing light.

A sharp crash reverberated overhead, and my gaze flew to the ceiling. *Son of a vampire*. They were here.

My pulse took off again, a pounding staccato vibrating my entire chest. A thundering boom shook the ceiling above us as dirt rained down on our heads.

What the heck was going on up there?

I couldn't sit here and do nothing. I brushed the dirt out of my hair and swept my hand over my face.

As if Sammarah had read my mind, she jumped to her feet and raced toward the ladder. I leapt up and caught her wrist before she reached the first rung. Shaking my head violently, I mouthed, "No." If anyone was going up there, it was me.

"I promised Declan to watch you," I whispered.

"No. We promised to take care of each other."

My grip around her arm loosened, and I nodded as mutual understanding passed between us. Neither of us was willing to let Declan die today. She began to climb, and I hurried right after her.

As I neared the hatch, the clash of metal against metal rang out above us. Sammarah quickened her pace and swung the trapdoor open, crawling out into the closet. After the dank hole, the air seemed fresh in comparison.

Grunts and shouts carried through the corridor into the small bedroom. Sammarah moved toward the door, but I caught her arm. I put my hand up and mouthed, "Wait."

Footsteps thundered down the hall, and a terrible scream sent goose bumps racing over every inch of my skin. I was hoping to sneak into my room and grab the gun from my backpack, but it was too late for that.

I barreled by Sammarah and ran out into the living room. Declan was pinned to the ground, a towering angel with enormous wings looming over him. His sword was raised in the air, poised to thrust.

"No!" I screamed and pummeled into the angel's wide back. It was like hitting a brick wall. The golden haired giant peered down at me over his shoulder and snarled.

But it was all the distraction Declan needed. He flew up and punched his fist *into* the angel's chest. I hurtled out of the way, landing on the upturned couch as the behemoth staggered back.

Declan's maroon eyes glowed with a deep crimson hue. Blood covered his face and stained his t-shirt and jeans. My line of sight followed the trail of blood to his hand where something pulsated in the dim light.

My hand flew to my mouth as I gasped. I turned to the angel who was splayed out across the floor to confirm my fears. A fist sized gaping hole swelled from his chest.

Declan spat and released the heart. It bounced across the floor, landing next to the angel's head. A growl reverberated in Declan's throat, chilling me to the bone. "I told you both not to come up here."

I spun around to find Sammarah a few feet behind me, clutching onto the wall for support. Dark sunken eyes stared unbelieving, her skin as white as the fallen angel's wings.

"We have to get out of here now. More will come if they're not on their way already." Declan reached for me, but I recoiled, his fingers still covered in blood. Hurt flashed across his blazing irises, but he quickly schooled his expression back to normal. "Liv, Mom, we have to go—now."

His mother peeled herself off the wall and raced to her bedroom. I grabbed my backpack from the extra room where I found Duke huddled under the bed. *Scaredy-dog.*

When I returned to the sitting room, the fire in Declan's eyes had simmered. His expression softened when he saw me. He exhaled a slow breath. "I'm sorry you had to see that."

Why had it bothered me so much? I hated the angels—what did it matter if he killed one? He was protecting us after all. And yet, there was something about the brutality of the whole thing that would forever be seared in my brain.

"It's okay," I finally rasped out. "Where will we go?"

The muscles in his jaw contracted. "I'm not sure yet—far. Bariel said my father was looking for me. He can't find me, not now."

"We have to go back north into vampire territory. Aren't the angels banned from there?"

He shrugged. "The divide is sketchy, the pact loose at best. But it's probably our best option now."

Sammarah appeared with an armful of papers and the leather-bound book Declan had found earlier. Her long dark hair was wild, curls tumbling over her shoulders. *So that's where Declan had gotten it from.*

"Let me get a bag for all that, Mom." He disappeared around the corner, leaving me with the mysterious woman.

She held the pages tight to her chest as she regarded me. The vacant look was back. "I'm glad my son found you. You will be important. The two of you will do great things together long after I'm gone."

My head whipped back as if I'd been slapped. "E-excuse me?"

A knowing smirk split her lips, and she rocked back and forth on her heels like a kid dying to spill a secret.

Declan rounded the corner into the sitting room with a duffel bag over his shoulder. "I grabbed a few things from your bath-room and closet. I hope it's okay."

She gave her son a warm smile and took the bag. The three of us traipsed out of the house, and it was only then I noticed the destruction. Upturned furniture blocked the doorway, shards of splintered wood scattered across the carpeting. A gaping hole stretched across the wall dividing the entry from the living room, and the door hung loose from its hinges.

I hadn't seen any other angel bodies and for a brief moment I wondered how many there had been.

Declan hurried us down the front steps, and my eyes landed on the black Harley. My heart sank.

"How are we all going to fit?"

"Oh, we're not taking that death trap, dear." Sammarah's hand brushed my shoulder as she passed by me. She walked over to the garage and heaved the metal door open. A small silver compact appeared behind stacks of brown boxes. "We'll take this."

Declan chuckled. "A true solar-powered car. Nice. You don't see many of those these days."

I wanted to say you don't see many of any cars these days, but I kept my mouth shut for once.

"I bought it before all of this started. I never thought the vampires would find a way to block out the sun."

I guess that part hadn't been foretold…

Declan began to clear the boxes as his mom fiddled with the keys. "If I leave it outside for a few days, I can get it to run, even with this cloudy sky. But now that Declan is here, we won't have to worry about that." She patted his shoulder and handed him the keys. "Maybe you should drive."

"I was about to suggest the same thing." He clicked the key fob, unlocking the back doors for Duke and me. I slid in and tried to get comfortable with Duke taking up the majority of the backseat.

Sammarah settled into the passenger side, still clutching her papers to her chest. Declan held his hands out and brilliant white light shot out of his palms, bathing the car in a warm golden hue.

For a second, all the thoughts swarming in my brain ceased. A sense of utter tranquility came over me. I closed my eyes, relishing the serene moment.

Declan jumped into the car and revved the engine, shattering the peace. Anxiety, fear and unease bombarded my brain, back in full force. I squeezed my eyes shut to block it out, but it was no use. I sucked in a breath and leaned my head back. A warm wet tongue slid across my face, and I couldn't help the small grin that tugged at my lips.

Duke always knew how to make me smile. I sat up, leaning forward between the two front seats. "So where to?"

Declan pulled out of the driveway, veering the car toward the highway. "I guess we'll play it by ear."

"Don't be silly, dear." Sammarah shuffled through the pages in her lap. "I know exactly where we're going." She pulled one out, and I recognized it from the board I'd first discovered in the closet. It looked like some sort of map. "We're going to find the sakra lampiada."

"The shield of light?" I choked out.

"Why of course, Liv. It's up to us to save mankind."

~

KEEP READING for a sneak peek at Blood & Rebellion, releasing in November 2018.

DO you want to be the first to find out when Blood & Rebellion is released? Sign up to G.K. DeRosa's mailing list to get sneak peeks, and bonuses and be the first to know when it's out! www.gkderosa.com

IF YOU ENJOYED WINGS & Destruction, I would be ever so thankful if you left a review. It doesn't have to be long, just a few words is great. I love getting feedback from my readers! Thanks for being a fan, and I hope you had as much fun reading the book as I did writing it.

~ G.K.

SNEAK PEEK OF BLOOD & REBELLION

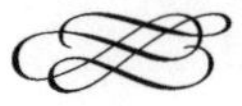

hapter 1

THREE HUNDRED AND fifty-five days ago the world went to hell. Literally. Now here I was, my fingers firmly entwined with those of the enemy.

"You okay?" Declan craned his neck over his shoulder and gave my arm a tug.

"Yeah," I panted as I trudged up the steep incline. The narrow passage didn't allow for side-by-side walking. Declan's mom, Sammarah, took the lead and somehow I'd ended up at the tail end of our little expedition through the unnerving catacombs.

I sucked in a breath of thick stale air as the terrain suddenly dipped downward. I squirmed out of Declan's hold and brushed my hands against the rough limestone rock on either side of us. The last thing I needed was to tumble down the decline and smack right into Declan. The *drip drip* of trickling water echoed across the narrow divide as we descended deeper into the fathomless underground cave.

"How much further, Mom?"

Sammarah abruptly stopped, holding the crude map up to focus her flashlight on it. "Shouldn't be too much longer."

I rolled my eyes. That's what she'd been saying for hours. Not for the first time in the past week, I questioned my sanity for following her. This was the third location we'd searched in the past seven days on our journey north. She was convinced this was where we'd find the mythical shield of light.

Just like she had been at the past two spots.

And yet, I kept following her. Having some sort of mission, however insane, was the only thing that kept me going. Did I really think some magical shield was going to save us from the vampires and angels? No. Then again, until a year ago, I didn't think angels or vampires were real either.

Declan halted, and I smashed right into his broad shoulders.

"Sorry," I muttered as I held onto his waist to steady myself.

He shone his flashlight over his mom's head revealing a rock wall in front of her. "Dead end," he huffed.

"I don't understand." She stared at the map as if it would suddenly divulge some hidden information.

"Maybe we should head back." It would be dark soon, and I didn't like the idea of Duke alone in the car for too long. We were in vampire territory now, and nothing good happened after dark.

"No. I know it's here." She turned the map around and around, scrutinizing it from all different angles. "Let me see the flashlight, Declan."

He handed it over, but it slid right through her trembling fingers, and fell to the rocky ground with a crash. Sooty darkness blanketed the passageway. I reached out for Declan, the sudden black taking my breath away.

Images of being trapped underground and buried alive flashed through my mind, my lungs constricting as my hands flailed searching for a familiar body. "Declan!"

"It's okay. I'm right here." An arm snaked around my waist and pulled me into his side. A brilliant white light lit up the claustrophobic space, and I could breathe again.

Declan raised his hand over his head, and a warm glow emanated from his palm.

Now I felt stupid for overreacting.

"What's that?" Sammarah cried out.

"What?" Declan spun toward her, taking me along with him.

"Shine your light over here." She ran her hand over the limestone rock, and a blue symbol appeared etched into the stone.

"What the heck is that?" I released my hold on Declan and moved toward the wall to stand next to Sammarah.

Her eyes widened as she stared at the strange mark. Dropping her bag to the ground, she hastily flipped through the stacks of papers. All of "her work" as she called it. She stopped on an old yellowing sheet and pointed. "This is it!"

I peered over her shoulder at the pages of ancient writing. I couldn't make out a thing, but the drawing was an exact match to the one carved into the rocks. It looked like a family crest with a pair of wings shooting out of it. The center part was divided into four sections and inside each segment was an image—a heart, book, sword and shield.

"What does this mean?"

Sammarah turned to me with a huge grin. "It means we've found it."

"The *sakra lampiada*?" Declan asked, moving closer.

"Not quite. I believe I may have misinterpreted the ancient translations, but we are definitely on the right path."

My shoulders slumped, and I let out a groan. *What the heck does that mean?*

"Patience, child." Sammarah pushed her dark curls out of her eyes and ran her hand over the wall. The symbol pulsated with life as her palm brushed over it.

My knees suddenly trembled, and my hands shot out to keep myself from falling. It took me a second to realize the tremor wasn't coming from within me. The entire passageway shook.

"Mom, watch out!" Declan yanked her out of the way just as an avalanche of rocks crashed to the ground.

I clung onto the side of the wall, the landslide setting off a cloud of debris that temporarily obstructed my sight. Declan and Sammarah stood beside me, both brushing dirt and rock fragments off their clothes.

"Look!" Sammarah pointed to the dead end. The symbol lit up, a bright blue glow bathing the cavern. The rock wall slid open.

My jaw nearly dropped to the floor. Before Declan could stop her, Sammarah darted through the opening.

"Mom, wait." He grabbed my hand and tugged me along behind him.

Could this really be it? A hidden cavern buried thousands of feet underground seemed like the ideal place to hide a mythical shield that could save the world. I held my breath as we followed Sammarah into the secret chamber.

A narrow rock formation sprang up from the center of a crystal clear turquoise body of water, creating a sort of bridge. At the end of the path, right in the middle of the glowing lagoon stood a pedestal. Thousands of shimmering stalactites hung from the ceiling like icicles in a winter wonderland. I tilted my head back to admire the glittering mineral spikes.

Sammarah was already half way across the bridge by the time I stopped staring. Her footsteps echoed within the cavernous space drawing my attention back to her quick movements.

"Mom, be careful," Declan shouted.

She didn't even turn around. It was like she was in a trance, her feet leading the way completely without her control.

Declan raced after her, and I ran after him. The minute I stepped on the bridge, I felt something. A wave of goose bumps rippled over my skin, like the air was charged with electricity. Every single hair on the back of my neck stood at attention.

"Do you feel that?"

Declan craned his neck back but kept moving. "Feel what?"

"I don't know. Something weird."

Sammarah's footsteps stopped, and I glanced ahead around Declan's large frame. She was hunched over whatever was on that pedestal. A wild giggle burst out of her mouth, reverberating across the limestone walls.

Declan reached her side and placed his hand on her shoulder. "What is it?"

I sprinted to catch up to them.

A sizable gold box sat atop the limestone base. I got on my tiptoes and peered over Declan's shoulder. The same symbol that had been etched on the wall was engraved on the golden encasing. There was no keyhole, no seam along the edges. Nothing that would provide an opening. Sammarah pressed her palm against the image and the ethereal glow lit up the chamber.

The gilded container unsealed, and the lid popped open.

My heart deflated. "That doesn't look like a shield to me."

A manic smile twisted Sammarah's lips. "Don't you see? This is only the beginning." She pulled a thick leather-bound book from the box and held it tight against her chest.

"What is it?" asked Declan. His gaze darted from his mother to the book and back to me.

I tried to school my features, but I was pretty sure his mom had lost it. Sammarah's mental state bounced back and forth between lucidity and insanity faster than a ping-pong ball.

"It's a sign that we're on the right track." She lifted the book up, revealing the worn brown cover. Elaborate golden scribbles surrounded the same symbol we'd seen everywhere.

"What does that mean? Is it Aramaic?" I asked. Sammarah's cryptic answers were really starting to annoy me.

Declan shook his head. "No. It's even older." His brows furrowed as he scrutinized the strange characters.

She pointed at the symbol. "It's the seal of the *divina sanguine*.

And it will lead us to the shield."

"Divine blood?" asked Declan.

She nodded, her eyes glassy. "It's the symbol of the blood that runs through my veins." She pressed her hand to her heart and smiled.

I wanted to believe her. She had led us to this underground cavern after all. That couldn't have been a coincidence, but divine blood? "So where do we go now?"

"The book will tell us all we need to know."

Chapter 2

"Do you think any of this could be true?"

Declan glanced over his shoulder to the backseat. Sammarah's head leaned against the headrest, a peaceful smile on her face. Duke lay across her lap, snoring contentedly. Declan blew out a sharp breath. "I don't know." His grip tightened on the steering wheel of the little electric car. "You saw what happened back there. She opened a door in a rock wall for god's sake—with a wave of her hand."

I nodded, the weight of his words heavy in the air. As insane as all of this sounded, it was true. Sammarah had some sort of magical powers. There was no other explanation. "Do you believe in magic?"

"No."

"Then how do you explain all of this?"

"Maybe she really is from this chosen bloodline. It's not magic, it's her destiny."

"So you believe in all of this now?" Up until a few hours ago, Declan had been as skeptical as I was.

He lowered his voice and turned his head to face me. "Before we left the catacombs, I touched the divine seal." He winced as if the memory were painful.

"And?"

"Nothing happened. No light, no ground shaking, no avalanche—nothing. It only reacted to her."

Hmm... I hadn't even thought to test it out myself. Declan had Sammarah's blood running through his veins and if anyone should've been able to access it, it should've been him. Unless whoever created the symbol had specifically designed it to ward off angels. Which definitely made sense.

"It's because you're an angel. Isn't this shield supposed to be a fail safe? It's to be used by a human against the immortals."

He grimaced, his shoulders slumping. "Yeah, I guess." He averted his gaze back to the dark road ahead. "It's just... I'm part human and I'm her son after all."

A pang jabbed me in the chest. I'd never fully realized it until now. Declan wanted to be human. Why he'd wish for such a dire fate I didn't understand.

His hand rested on the gearshift. I reached over and placed mine on top of his, giving it a squeeze. "Listen, with the way things turned out, you're lucky you're on the winning side. Trust me."

"It doesn't feel like I'm on the winning side of anything."

Silence swept through the car as I thought of something to say —anything to make him feel better. Nothing came to mind. I hated the angels and the vampires. They'd taken everything from me—my parents, Asher, my whole world. There wasn't a single redeeming quality that could bring him comfort.

"Let's stop here." He pointed at a sprawling suburban community off the highway and took the exit ramp.

We were somewhere in southern Pennsylvania, but I wasn't sure where. Our first two stops in search of the shield had taken us through Maryland. Who knew where the book would take us next?

Declan stopped in front of a two-story colonial home with ivory columns and a red brick façade. Somehow it had remained fairly intact while the surrounding houses had entire roofs blown off. There was no rhyme or reason to the immortals' destruction.

We trudged inside, Declan carrying his sleeping mom and Duke at my heels. We'd spent every night over the past week in a different place. I was tired of all the traveling and would've given anything to be back home in my own bed.

Except my home didn't exist anymore. Not really anyway.

The basement was still standing—or at least it had been when Asher and I left, but a house without the people you love, isn't really a home. Asher's face flashed across my mind, his dull green eyes starred in most of my nightmares. What had the angels done to him? I struggled to convince myself the person I knew died long before Declan had killed him. It was the only way I could live with myself. And Declan.

"You okay?" He appeared at my side as I dragged my feet into the living room.

"Yeah. Just tired." I noticed his mom was no longer in his arms. "You found the bedrooms?"

He motioned his head to the left. "Down that corridor to the stairs. There are three of them and a bathroom up there."

I nodded and slumped down on the couch.

"You're not going to bed?" He stood in front of me, dark locks nearly covering his maroon eyes.

"Not yet." I stared at the huge flat screen TV, wishing we had power. I missed my old TV shows like crazy. It would've been nice to have something to escape into.

Declan sat beside me, wrapping his fingers around mine. His palm began to glow and waves of soothing energy flowed up my arm. Zapping me with angel light had kind of become our thing. A small sigh escaped my parted lips.

"It's like bottled sunshine," I whispered.

"What?" Declan chuckled.

"Your power. It's amazing. It's like I'm sitting on a sandy beach in the Caribbean without a care in the world." As I said the words, it hit me. This. This was Declan's gift. His angelic healing power was extraordinary. I squeezed his hand and glanced up. Piercing maroon irises fixed on me. My breath hitched, as it had a tendency of doing lately when Declan gave me that look. "I'm glad you're part angel."

His eyes widened, breaking the lock they had on mine. "I didn't think I'd ever hear that from you."

I shrugged. "I guess I'd forgotten some of the perks that came along with it. Like this one." I glanced down at our glowing intertwined hands.

A big smile flashed across his face, one that actually reached his eyes. It reminded me of the old Declan, the funny, cocky one I'd first met.

"Liv, there's something I need to tell you."

I straightened, the tone in his voice ominous. "Okay…"

Duke barked, his nails clicking across the hardwood floor as he raced to the front door. Declan jumped up. His expression tensed as he strained to hear whatever Duke had heard.

"Dammit," he growled.

"What?"

"Looters outside." He released me and crept toward the door. I hurried behind him, but he raised his hand. "Stay there," he mouthed.

I leaned against the flowery wallpaper, craning my head around the corner to get a better view of the entrance. Duke barked and growled, his claws scratching at the door. Declan moved beside him and peered out the peephole.

The sound of approaching footsteps sent my heart rate on overdrive. Declan backed away from the door just as a gunshot rang out in the heavy silence. He grabbed Duke and yanked him back as splintered wood torpedoed across the fancy foyer. I dropped down, throwing my arms over my head to protect from the flying debris.

The door flew open, smacking against the wall and two men with rifles filled the entryway. Duke bared his fangs, his hackles raised as Declan pushed himself off the floor. Shards of wood stuck out of his chest, trickles of blood dripping down his shirt.

I clapped my hand over my mouth to keep from screaming.

The bigger guy pointed the rifle at Declan. "Give us everything you've got."

The pungent odor of booze permeated the stale air, reaching all the way to my tucked away hiding spot.

Duke began barking again, and Declan raised his hands. "No need for the guns. I'll give you whatever you want."

"Where are the other two?" The guy who wore a backward baseball cap nodded toward the grand staircase.

"What other two?" Declan folded his arms across his chest.

"Don't lie to me, boy." The big guy stepped into the light, revealing a gruesome scar across his eye and cheek. "We saw you drive in here—you and two women. We'll take that car off your hands too."

My heart pounded against my ribcage, all too eager to escape its prison. Duke continued barking, the frantic rhythm echoing through my eardrums.

"Shut that dog up or I will," hissed blue baseball cap guy, turning his rifle on Duke. "The vamps are gonna hear him and kill us all."

No.

"Duke, enough." Declan lowered his hands and yanked on his collar. "There's no need to kill anyone tonight. As for the women with me, they're asleep upstairs." He moved away from the staircase and toward the living room. "I'll get everything you need, and you can be on your way."

What was he doing? He couldn't let those scumbags take our supplies, especially not our car.

Once the foyer was clear, I tiptoed after them. Peering around the corner to the living room, I found Declan filling a bag with food and water. The men had lowered their weapons, but scar guy still had a firm hold on the handle of his rifle. I eyed my backpack sitting on the couch and cursed. If I could only reach my gun somehow…

Declan continued to pile more supplies into the bag as Duke kept an eye on the strangers. He stood in between them and Declan, his muscles tense, a low growl vibrating in his throat.

I shifted positions, and the old wood floorboards creaked. *Son of a vampire!* Duke's ears perked up, his head turning in my direction. The man with the scar followed his gaze and raised his weapon.

"Come out here now, or I'll shoot," he snarled.

"It's nothing," shouted Declan.

The man took a step toward me. I stopped breathing.

ALSO BY G.K. DE ROSA

The Guardian Series

Wilder: The Guardian Series

Wilder Destiny

Wilder Revelation

Wilder Legacy

Wilder: The Guardian Series The Complete Collection

The Hybrid Trilogy

Magic Bound

Immortal Magic

Beyond Magic

The Vampire Prophecy

Dark Fates

Dark Divide

Dark Oblivion

ACKNOWLEDGMENTS

A huge and wholehearted thank you to my dedicated readers! I could not do this without you. I love hearing from you and your enthusiasm for the characters and story. You are the best!

A special thank you to my loving and supportive husband who always understood my need for escaping into a good book (or TV show!). He inspires me to try harder and push further every day. And of course my mother who is the guiding force behind everything I do and made me everything I am today. Without her, I literally could not write—because she's also my part-time babysitter! To my father who will always live on in my dreams. And finally, my son, Alexander, who brings an unimaginable amount of joy and adventure to my life everyday.

A big thank you to my new talented graphic designer, Sanja Gombar, for creating a beautiful book cover. A special thank you to my dedicated beta readers/fellow authors Jena, Kristin and Tiea who have been my sounding board on everything from cover ideas, blurbs, and story details. And all of my beta readers who gave me great ideas, caught spelling errors, and were all around amazing.

Thank you to all my family and friends (especially you, Robin Wiley!) and new indie author friends who let me bounce ideas off of them and listened to my struggles as an author and self-publisher. I appreciate it more than you all will ever know.

G.K.

ABOUT THE AUTHOR

USA Today Bestselling Author, G.K. De Rosa has always had a passion for all things fantasy and romance. Growing up, she loved to read, devouring books in a single sitting. She attended Catholic school where reading and writing were an intense part of the curriculum, and she credits her amazing teachers for instilling in her a love of storytelling. As an adult, her favorite books were always young adult novels, and she remains a self-proclaimed fifteen year-old at heart. When she's not reading, writing or watching way too many TV shows, she's traveling and eating around the world with her family. G.K. DeRosa currently lives in South Florida with her real life Prince Charming, their son and fur baby, Nico, the German shepherd.

Contact me:

Website: www.gkderosa.com and www.wilderbook.com

Email: gkderosa@wilderbook.com

Facebook: www.facebook.com/wilderbookseries and www.facebook.com/gkderosa

Twitter: @vampgirl923

Goodreads: G.K. DeRosa

Instagram: GK DeRosa

Made in the USA
Middletown, DE
14 December 2018